SOUND OF THE BUGLE

Sound of the Bugle

The Adventures of Hans Schmidt

Daniel R. Burow

Drawings by
Barry F. Smith and Associates

Publishing House
St. Louis   London

Concordia Publishing House, St. Louis, Missouri
Concordia Publishing House Ltd., London, E. C. 1
Copyright © 1973 Concordia Publishing House
Library of Congress Catalog Card No. 72-91152
ISBN 0-570-03145-1
MANUFACTURED IN THE UNITED STATES OF AMERICA

To Marcia
and our own Klaus, Hans, and Maria

CONTENTS

SOUND OF THE BUGLE

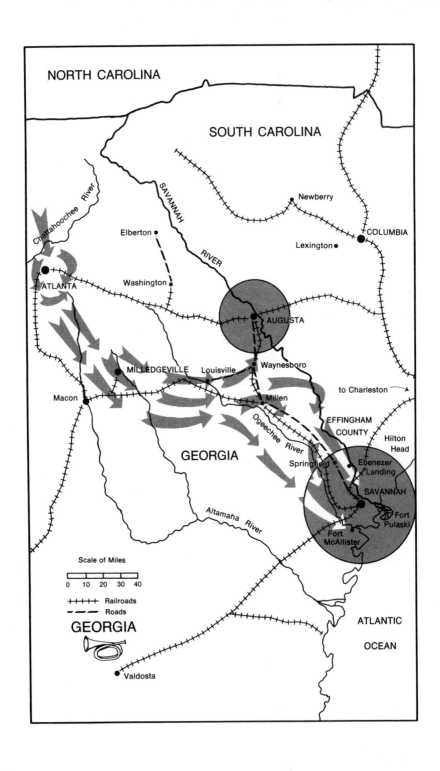

NORTH CAROLINA

SOUTH CAROLINA

Newberry

COLUMBIA

Elberton

Lexington

SAVANNAH

Washington

RIVER

ATLANTA

AUGUSTA

Chattahoochee River

MILLEDGEVILLE

Louisville

Waynesboro

Macon

Millen

to Charleston

EFFINGHAM
COUNTY

Hilton
Head

Ogeechee River

GEORGIA

Springfield

Ebenezer
Landing

SAVANNAH

Fort
Pulaski

Altamaha River

Fort
McAllister

Scale of Miles

0   10   20   30   40

+++++ Railroads
- - - Roads

GEORGIA

Valdosta

ATLANTIC

OCEAN

1. Flight from Prussian Glory

At the far corner of my writing desk stand nine and a half tin soldiers. Eight, with muskets leaning against their right shoulder, are grouped around a brass cannon. Off to one side the ninth presses a bugle to his lips. Opposite him stands what remains of the tenth — the stumps of two legs protruding upwards from their metal base.

Each time I sit in their presence these nearly-ten survivors of my adventures will not be restrained from repeating to me every last detail of the story. But when others are present they always turn mute. Therefore, since only I can hear them, I shall attempt to put in writing the story these sentinels have so often repeated to me.

To begin their story at the beginning, my name is Hans Schmidt. The name may be familiar to you not, I'm afraid, because of anything I have done, but because in the land of my birth we Hans Schmidts are as numerous as sausage links.

Yet I do have one claim to fame. On my mother's side I am the great, great grandson of Baron von Rohr, a general in the army of Frederick the Great. This never overwhelmed any of the boys I met in America, but then they hadn't spent their early years in Germany growing up in the military kingdom of Prussia as I had. Then too, by some conspiracy among historians, the Baron never received more than scant note even in German history books.

As early as I can remember, having the Baron for an ancestor inspired in me a fierce determination to follow in his steps. As I sit here at my desk, the tin sentinels recall for me all the details of that determination.

It was late April, the year 1859 — a few days after my 11th birthday. A faint tinge of green among the trees already harbored the first sign of spring as Klaus and I headed home from school.

"Can't you hurry up?" he scolded in his bossiest big-brother manner.

"I am hurrying," I answered in my sauciest little-brother manner. "My legs aren't as long as yours."

"Well, you can run, can't you?"

"When I want to." I continued marching in evenly-measured strides, the way I saw soldiers do, and counted out the cadence. "One, two, three, four. One, two, three, four."

"Do you have to march all the time? You're not a soldier yet, you know."

"I've got to practice — three, four."

"Oh, I can just see you as a soldier! You'll be a pastor just like Father wants, only you'll have seven devils in you!"

"A pastor? Two, three, four. Never! Two, three, four. Someday I'll wear one of those blue uniforms with the shiny gold buttons."

"You'll wear Father's handprint on your bottom if you don't hurry up! He's probably home already, and you know what he'll say if we're late."

I stuck to my soldiering, so Klaus gave up on me and ran ahead.

For a while the Baron and I camped with our troops at the side of the road. Suddenly we heard a shrill bugle call up ahead. We mounted our steeds and, with sabers drawn and the spikes atop our helmets glistening in the sun, sped toward the sound of the bugle.

When I charged into the parlor, Klaus already had his violin in hand. Mother was sitting on the sofa, her flute on her lap and little Maria cuddled next to her. Father was impatiently tapping his fingers on the cello.

Except for the finger tapping the parlor was so quiet I could hear my pores breathe. They panted and wheezed nervously until after some minutes Father shattered the silence.

"Well, Hans, did you forget this was Thursday?" He paused as if expecting an answer. "How much time do I get with the family anyway? How often do we get to play together?" He picked up the sheaf of music and shook it at me. "This concerto is scored for piano. Or have you forgotten what a piano is?"

"You could make him take organ lessons," Klaus volunteered as my punishment.

I showed him my teeth. He knew how I hated the idea of organ lessons. Piano lessons were bad enough. But organ lessons! What would a soldier need with organ lessons?

"I suppose you'd work the bellows for me," I snapped.

His mouth curled up at the right corner. "Anything to see you play the organ!"

Father's face grew stern. "That's enough! Organ lessons aren't for punishment. They're a privilege, one that Hans doesn't appreciate yet." He set the cello aside. When he looked up, his eyes betrayed the dawn of a smile. "Anyway, where could we find an organ master to put up with his pranks?" He rubbed his nose thoughtfully as his mood softened noticeably. "Besides, we've another reason to wait with the organ lessons."

"What's that?" Klaus wanted to know.

"Well, it's not definite yet. So until I reach my decision, let's just forget the matter."

Now I was curious. "Forget what?"

"*That* is a secret."

"But how can I forget a secret I don't even know?"

"How can you forget one you do know? Your tongue would remember it everywhere."

"Oh, Father, I can keep a secret!"

"Yes, with my help. So I'll help."

"Oh, good!"

"By not telling you. Now, on with the concerto!"

I groaned but didn't pursue the matter further, because

when Father held a secret, not all the crowbars in the world could pray it loose. But as my fingers stumbled over the keyboard, falling on many an unwary note, I kept wondering what it could be.

In the days that followed I kept my eyes and ears alert for clues. But a soldier has to be flexible. So I kept my mind from being absorbed by just the secret. I set it to work also on concocting something special for Klaus — to pay him back for bringing up the organ lessons. He had started life 11 months ahead of me, and he had used the entire head start inventing ways to be ornery. So I had to find something just right, something I could be sure to enjoy while being equally sure he wouldn't.

Mother put me to the task of nailing down several loose floorboards in my bedroom. When my chore was completed I wandered into Klaus's room for inspiration.

As always, his room was in immaculate order. Not so much as a wrinkle in his bedspread, or a dresser drawer left even slightly ajar! Even his slippers were lined up toe to toe precisely one step from the bed. He was so thorough and methodical!

I could see him now going through his nightly ritual. First, he'd light the lamp on the bedside table, then undress and carefully fold his clothes over the back of the cane chair. Then, pouring water into the basin, he'd gingerly pat some on his face and gingerly pat it right back off as clean as before onto the towel. Then he'd slip into his nightgown and sit ever so exactly on the edge of the bed to remove his shoes. Last, he'd slide his feet into the slippers placed so precisely within reach of his outstretched legs. It always amazed me how he could move so slowly through each step of this ritual until his feet slipped into those slippers. Then with a sudden bound he'd be off like a gazelle to kiss Mother goodnight.

Recalling this ritual filled me with disgust but not with even a hint of inspiration. I was turning to leave when a nail dropped from my hand. Whether the work of devil or muse, I don't know, but the nail landed smack in one of the slippers. I stooped down to fetch it. Suddenly this – this *thing* started whirling my head with a madness. And the hammer started pounding on the nail. It pounded nail after nail while the slippers sprouted metallic roots deep into the floorboards.

From downstairs Mother called, "Hans, aren't you done yet? It's time for Maria's nap."

The veins in my temple swelled. "Almost, Mother." *Bang! Bang! Bang!* "Now it's done!" Indeed it was.

Like the slippers, the remainder of the afternoon refused to budge, no matter how much I tried to hurry it. Whenever I ran into Klaus I had to giggle. He'd frown and say, "What's the matter with you?" And my not answering him made his hair bristle.

At long last the moment came. We had finished our bed-time prayers, and Klaus and I headed upstairs for bed while Mother sang Maria to sleep on the sofa. I lagged well behind him and crouched near the top of the stairs to watch through the banister as he disappeared into his darkened room.

Then began the unvarying ceremony. He lit the lamp, undressed, carefully draped his clothes over the chair, filled the basin, washed his immaculate face, put on his nightgown, and sat down on the edge of the bed. *Thud!* One shoe. *Thud!* The other. His legs reached out for the slippers.

I clamped a hand over my nose to muffle a snicker.

His toes felt their way forward to the tip of his slippers. He heaved a sigh, then his body bounded forward – but not his feet!

"Aaach!" *Blump!*

Klaus lay sprawled on the floor, his eyes staring stupidly at the darkened hallway like a sleepwalker waking up in the middle of a crowded fish market. I giggled to myself: "Hans Schmidt strikes again!"

He sat up to examine his slippers. His fingers felt inside, and I headed for my room, still struggling to smother my snickers.

"H-a-n-s-!"

I tried to shut my door quietly, but then I heard him coming on like a steam engine. I slammed the door the rest of the way and bolted it.

"Open up, Hans!" He rattled the knob, then started pounding and hollering. "Open up, Hans! You open this door!"

"Klaus! What's the matter with you?" came the hushed but earnest call from downstairs. "Maria's trying to sleep. Now not another sound, or your father will hear about this when he gets home."

Knowing that I was safe for now I uncovered my mouth but laughed so loud that I had to bury my head under the pillow to keep Mother from hearing me. Klaus rapped lightly on the wall, so I knew he had heard me and was warning me fair.

Next morning I left for school before either Klaus or Father came down for breakfast. I avoided Klaus all day and after school hurried home before he could catch me. But once home I had another problem: Father was there. Through the front door I could hear him in the parlor talking to Mother.

I slipped in by the back door and sat down in the hallway by the staircase. From there I could eavesdrop to learn Father's mood, and from there I could effect a hasty retreat if I had to. Soldiers must think of things like that!

Mother was speaking. "Are you sure the regent is planning to enforce the old draft laws?"

She wasn't talking about last night. That was good.

Father spoke next. "Yes, I'm sure. And that's just the beginning. When Wilhelm becomes king, he'll get us into a war with France or Austria. Maybe with both."

"But why?"

"For Prussian glory."

"Prussian glory! What do I want with glory, especially when it means shedding my children's blood?" Mother sounded like she was on the verge of tears.

"Don't worry, Mamma. He won't get a chance to shed *our* children's blood. Not now! My decision ends that!" Just then I saw Klaus's obnoxious head silhouetted on the opaque glass of the front door. In my hurry to get upstairs I tripped.

"Is that you, Klaus?" Father called.

I didn't answer. Father appeared in the parlor doorway. "Oh, it's you, Hans!" His brow knitted with furrows all the way up into his balding crown. "Well, what have you been up to?"

"Sir?" I stammered.

"Come now, you look like the cat that just cleaned out the goldfish bowl. What have you to tell me?"

"You mean about the slippers?"

"The slippers? Yes, well, I suppose so. What slippers?"

"Klaus didn't . . . tell . . . you?"

"No, but maybe you'd like to."

"Oh, no, sir!"

"Do anyhow."

The front door opened behind Father.

"Never mind for now. Klaus is here. I want to see you two in the parlor."

Klaus glared at me as he swept by. "Father, did Hans tell you what he did to my slippers? Last night . . . ."

"Klaus, I called you in here to discuss another matter."

"But, Father . . . ."

"Well, if you'd rather not hear my secret . . . ."

"Oh, no!" I pleaded. "Let's hear the secret."

Klaus sank onto the sofa utterly defeated.

"We're going to . . . ." Father paused as if to increase our suspense. "We're going to . . . ." Again he paused and smiled his teasing smile. "We're going . . . to . . . America."

"America?" I gasped.

"Going where?" Klaus asked with his jaw sagging down over his tie.

Father made no reply, just waited for the words to sink in. "America?" I repeated. "The land of savage Indians?" I looked at Mother. "Leave Germany?"

She nodded.

"Leave our home? And friends?"

"But why?" Klaus asked.

Mother said, "Well, you see, several weeks ago your father received a letter from a congregation near Savannah. One of their pastors died during a yellow-fever epidemic five years ago, and they've been without a second pastor since."

"Why don't they get one from America?" I asked.

"Well, maybe they don't have enough. Besides they want a pastor who can work with German-speaking people as well as English-speaking. And Father speaks both languages quite well. And, well, here . . . your father thinks he's not needed as much."

She continued her explanation but I wasn't listening anymore. Father was studying me and I was wondering if I showed fear. I had always prided myself on possessing bravery in heroic proportions. If I couldn't beat up every boy in my class, at least I wasn't afraid to challenge any of them. And I just knew that what I would dare on a battlefield one day was practically beyond belief. But tangling with savage Indians in the American jungle — somehow that seemed different.

"Why?" I repeated.

Mother looked startled; I must have interrupted her. "That's what I've been explaining, Hans."

Suddenly it came to me — the conversation I had overheard earlier! Of course! The whole thing was a plot to keep me from being a soldier! They were taking me away from Germany so I couldn't be drafted, so I would *have* to be pastor someday.

"No, you won't!" I said angrily.

Father and Mother looked at each other.

"You just want to keep me out of the army!"
Father's face grew red and his chest swelled. "Don't
you talk to us in that tone of voice!"

That ended the conversation.

Up in my bedroom I stared out the window. The more
my bitterness grew, the more also my determination.
I threw myself across the bed and growled between clenched
teeth: "If Father thinks he can keep me from being a soldier, he doesn't know Hans Schmidt!"

2. To the American Jungle

We sailed from Bremerhaven — and from any possibility
of my ever being a soldier; at least Father must have thought
so. Of course, he didn't know about the war clouds gathering even then over America.

At Liverpool we changed ships and set sail aboard the
Arago, a large side-wheel steamship with an iron hull and
two slender funnels stacked between its undersized masts.

One evening the captain invited us to his table for a late
supper. I had to stay in our cabin and watch Maria because
at dinner Klaus had pulled a chair out from behind me.
Father thought it was an accident. He didn't think it an
accident, though, when spreading my napkin I also spread
a bowl of turtle soup across Klaus's lap.

By suppertime Father wasn't angry anymore, but he
was not one to relent on punishment. Before leaving the
cabin he told me to take good care of Maria and not to
tease her, and to practice my English because he wanted
us all to speak English fluently by the time we reached
Savannah. He handed me the English book, then thought

better of it and said, "Oh, just for tonight maybe you'd rather entertain yourself with this book!" He produced a gilt-edged book with a red cover. "It's a story about a young pastor," he explained.

He just happened to have that book handy!

"And be good, Hans," Mother pleaded. "Please?"

When they had shut the cabin door, I shoved aside the books Father had given me and reached under the pillow for my favorite: *The Life of Frederick the Great*. It didn't mention the Baron, but it was loaded with pictures of soldiers and battles.

Little Maria was sitting on the lower bunk looking at a picture book, so I sprawled out on the bunk above her and read. Before long I was completely absorbed, having persuaded myself that a certain officer in one of the battle scenes was the Baron and that I was at his side riding at the head of the army. Soon I was so busy charging through the thunderous cannonade and wreaking havoc on the enemy's ranks that I didn't hear the cabin door open or feel the draft.

At last the heat of battle made me thirsty. I climbed down to fetch the canteen, and that's when I noticed that the door was open and Maria gone!

I looked out the door. No Maria. "Maria!" I called softly. No answer. I raced up the companionway to the deck.

"Maria!" Still no answer — only the churning of the paddle wheels.

I searched as far forward as the bridge that stretched between the two side-wheels, dividing the ship in half. I knew she couldn't have gone up there or the sailor at the wheel would have seen her. But he had his back to me and was quietly intent upon his business. So I tiptoed toward the stern, past the portside lifeboats and along the railing that curved around the stern deckhouse.

"Hans!" came the teasing tone of a three-year-old. There she stood — by the rail on the starboard side of the deckhouse. The rail was almost as high as she but was wide open underneath, affording her no protection if she lost her balance.

"Maria!" I half screeched. Quick as a wink she grabbed onto the rail, swung under it to the seaward side, turned toward me, and giggled.

I froze in my tracks. If she should lose her grip and fall overboard . . . ! "Maria!" I called desperately.

She giggled again and started sliding playfully by her arms along the rail. I tried to approach her, but she grabbed onto a rail post, leaned back out over the deep, and giggled again that girly giggle.

I didn't take another step. "Please God!" I pleaded. "Don't let her fall! What would Father and Mother say?"

"Please, Maria, come to Hans. I'll give you something."

"What?" she asked saucily.

"Something nice."

"No. Come and catch me," she said with growing excitement.

"No, Maria! I don't want to play now. Come here!"

"No!" Now she was pouting.

I heard someone behind me whisper, "Need help?"

I turned around and saw a sailor pressing himself against the side of the deckhouse. "Please!" I begged.

"Just keep talking to her quietly," he told me.

"Hans, who are you talking to?" Maria wanted to know.

"To you, Maria. Hang on tight. P-l-e-a-s-e!"

The sailor stole along the stern rail until he was within a few feet of her. Suddenly she saw him and stiffened. He stopped. She eyed him suspiciously for a long time. Neither of them moved. Finally Maria took her eyes off him, leaned back, and looked down at the ocean sliding beneath her. The sailor lunged at her and caught her right hand, causing her to jump with fright and lose her footing. In an instant she was dangling over the water. I rushed forward to grab her by the skirt, but her legs flailed the air so, I couldn't get a grip and was forced to listen helplessly to her pathetic screams.

The sailor bumped me aside as he reached down with his other arm and grabbed her by the back of the skirt. She struggled so desperately, though, that he couldn't pull her on board. "Oh, God!" I groaned. Then with one great heave the sailor swung her over the rail onto the deck.

She and I both sobbed as I hugged her.

"We had better tell your parents," the sailor said.

"Oh, no, please! I'm supposed to be taking care of her," I pleaded.

"Is this how you do it?"

"I'll do better. Please!"

"You'd better!" he said gravely.

"I will, I promise."

He rubbed his jaw for a minute. "All right. But remember, I have your word. Come on, I'll take you to your cabin." He carried Maria the whole way and tucked her in her bunk. Before leaving he insisted I lock the cabin door so he could hear it lock.

Later, as I let the family in, Father said, "You didn't miss much, Hans, but, then, I guess it must've been a dull evening for you too."

I laid down the English book and looked at Maria, who was fast asleep. "Yes," I answered, "quite dull."

The next morning Father repented of denying me the chance to meet the captain. He took me to the bridge and introduced me.

"Ah," said the captain, thumping his pipe on his hand, "the one who wants to be a soldier! I understand you're already quite a marksman — with a bowl of soup."

I grinned an embarrassed grin.

"Well, lad, have you ever thought of being a ship's captain?"

"No, sir."

"You should. Really, it's just the thing for a person

who likes to work with, ah, a *fluid* medium. Say, why not stay up here awhile and captain the ship?"

I could hardly refuse such an offer. So I stayed and felt like I was in control of the world. Then the wind picked up.

I watched as the ship's bow lifted high into the leaden sky then began to fall until it knifed deep into the sea. The ocean rushed up at me, and I thought we were plunging to the bottom. But suddenly the onrushing water slowed, then stopped, then receded until it completely disappeared and once again the ship's bow reached into the heavens.

So it went. Up and down. Into the clouds, beneath the sea. Flying into the clouds, slipping beneath the sea. Up and down. Clouds and sea. Up and down. Clouds and sea.

I mumbled something about Mother needing me and headed for the stern deckhouse. On the way I passed Klaus.

"Ha! Getting scared, brave soldier?" he sneered.

"Who says?"

"Who says? Your face says! It's pea green."

"Liar!"

"Well, if you're not seasick you'll be glad to hear we're having raw oysters for supper."

He hee-hawed as I clutched my stomach and raced down to the cabin. I didn't quite make it. And that was only the beginning. I stayed sick for days while Klaus never wasted a chance to torment me. Father and Mother wouldn't let him say anything, but he did it with looks. A smirk here, a gloat there.

I had no peace at all until the day someone pounded on the cabin door. Father opened it and in stumbled a sailor half carrying and half dragging a drenched Klaus.

Mother cried, "Oh God! What's the matter with him?"

I wondered if he was dead. Then he started to bawl, which answered my question.

"What happened?" Father demanded.

"This crazy bloke . . . ." The sailor looked at Mother.

"Sorry, Mum. I mean, this kid of yours was up on deck. And you know, Mum, it's awash half the time. Well, I was yelling at him to go below. I guess he couldn't hear me what with the wind and all. Then this here wave comes along and knocks him down and starts to wash him overboard. I grabs his arm just in time or he'd a been for the deep six."

That ended the smirks and the gloats. Also my sickness. And for the rest of the trip I regarded the sea almost as a friend.

Our first view of America came as something of a shock to me. Instead of a jungle I saw a forest of ship masts and, beyond them, New York's skyline crowded with buildings. A steady stream of barges floated down the Hudson to the accompaniment of locomotives chugging in the distance.

Ashore I was even more amazed. Horse-drawn trolleys. Hoards of peddlers pushing their carts. Store windows displaying more wares than I knew existed. And from our hotel window that night row after row of gas lamps puncturing the darkness along the still-busy thoroughfares.

"Is this what Georgia is like?" I asked Father.

"Oh," he said, "I think Georgia will give us a surprise or two of its own!"

3. Foreigners We

Our ship to Savannah, a wooden sailing schooner from a bygone age, creaked continuously. Fortunately the ocean remained calm the whole way or surely the ship would have splintered into driftwood.

When we left the ocean's vastness behind us and sailed up the marshy estuary of the Savannah River, I felt relieved. And when we saw the brick walls of a new fort —

Fort Pulaski—on an island in the middle of the river, I began to feel almost enthusiastic about America.

Another 15 miles up the river and we reached Savannah, which I quickly discovered was not exactly New York. The harbor was busy enough, with crowds of slaves manhandling bales of cotton out of harbor warehouses into the holds of waiting ships, but the warehouses were hardly more than patchworks of brick on stone. At the top of the bluff on which the city was built the cobblestone streets leading up from the wharves turned to a white sand that even camels would have found difficult to walk on. And only a few blocks from the river the full impact of the sultry, subtropical heat hit us. Fortunately magnolias and oaks lined the streets, and every few blocks the main streets broadened into tree-shaded squares.

Our first real omen of things to come arrived the following day in the persons of Mr. and Mrs. Hanser. They drove us in a farm wagon from the hotel out to Effingham County.

"My husband is a deacon of the congregation," announced Mrs. Hanser. "He's a person you'll have to depend on heavily, Mr. Schmidt."

We soon learned that our parishioners always called their pastors "mister."

"Mr. Koenig, the pastor of one of our churches here in Savannah, and Mr. Dorow—you'll like him, a lovely young man, very agreeable, he's the head pastor out our way—well, they're both away just now, and so they asked Mr. Hanser and myself to fetch you all."

Mrs. Hanser flashed her sugary smile on and off as quickly and easily as a telegraph operator taps out dots and dashes.

"You all will just love it here, I know. You've got such wonderful people to work with. Did I tell you my husband cuts timber? Well, not really. He has boys to do the cutting, but he does all the hard work—you know, in his head. And what a head! Right, dear? Did I tell you he's a deacon?

Yes, I guess I did. Well, the pastors have always depended on him, and you will too, Mr. Schmidt. Oh, by the way, how was your trip? Good, I hope. Yes, you'll love it here. My, don't you have darling children! So quiet. We have a wonderful congregation."

She rarely stopped for breath and never for an answer, but her husband always nodded on cue.

"And wait 'til you see the parsonage. You all will just love it. Cute as a bug's ear. Right, honey? I went over and fixed it up yesterday morning, all by myself—no boys to help or nothing. Right, honey? The former tenants weren't very tidy, but it's all right now. Oh, I can hardly wait to see your faces when you see that house!"

I could hardly wait either. She went on that way hour after hour. I was soaked with perspiration, but she wasn't even warmed up.

Outside the city we passed rice plantations and large, stately plantation houses, one in a shady mulberry grove. Each mansion house we approached I thought, "This must be ours." But on we went through this low, flat country, and on went the torrid heat and Mrs. Hanser. For amusement I began comparing my view of the right horse with Mrs. Hanser's face. The likenesses were remarkable, subtracting the tail, of course.

The road entered densely wooded country of tall, spindly pines.

"Great for turpentine and lumber. Right, dear? Stretches for just miles and miles, I guess all the way up to Augusta maybe, and maybe farther. Oh, see that church? Ours once. Methodist now. That's the one I told you about before, but you all remember that, don't you? Of course you do."

From Savannah we had traveled north about fifteen miles when we crossed into Effingham County. Another half dozen miles and we turned off the Augusta Road onto a side road leading east toward the river. I hadn't seen any great mansion houses for a while and wondered why they would have built ours on this narrow lane with its towering walls of pine and amid neighbors whose houses were barely more than shacks.

We rounded a bend and came upon several oaks so massive and bearded with Spanish moss that they completely hid us from the light of the sun. The wagon stopped. "Well, what did I tell you?" Mrs. Hanser said. "What . . . did . . . I . . . tell you?"

"What?" Mother asked.

Mrs. Hanser pointed to the left side of the road, between some tall pines. "There!"

My eyes followed her gnarled finger and saw a sandy path leading through a split-rail fence overgrown with weeds and straggly azaleas. The path curved in front of a large wooden stable that seemed dwarfed by the surrounding pines, then veered off to the right to . . . . No, that was the stable to the right. Which meant that what I first thought was a stable had to be . . . a house!

Both had steep, gabled roofs that flattened out somewhat in the front to form a kind of porch. Yes, the first had to be a house. It stood several feet off the ground on little columns of bricks and had steps leading up to a porch. It had windows and a chimney, also some sort of smaller wooden building standing close behind it. Clearly all three buildings had never seen a paint brush, and clearly the first was a house in which people must have once actually lived.

"You told us about this?" Father asked.

"Told you? Ha, ha. Oh my, yes! Hard to believe, isn't it? Snug. Cozy. Didn't I tell you you'd love it?"

The truth began to dawn. "You mean this . . . is . . . ."

"The parsonage. Look, honey. Look at their faces! Didn't I tell you? They can't believe it."

And we couldn't.

The pallor of our faces in no way diminished Mrs. Hanser's enthusiasm as she conducted us on a grand tour of the estate. First we entered the house. In spite of the

roof's height at its peak, the house had no second story. It had only a parlor, three bedrooms, and a narrow hallway that ran from the front door directly to the back. I calculated that the parlor with its fireplace by the far wall was too small to allow for a piano. That was a plus. A bit of quick arithmetic told me Klaus and I would have to share the same bedroom, and this did nothing to endear me to America.

The building out back turned out to be a kitchen and store room. It had no stove, only an open hearth. Outside, about 20 feet from the kitchen, stood a well — no pump, just a well. While Mother looked like she was about to faint, Mrs. Hanser droned on about the quality of the water.

The yard was shaded by tall pines and a few pecan trees except for a cleared acre behind the outhouse. Across from the outhouse stood or leaned a heap which, Mrs. Hanser announced, was the chicken house.

Mr. Hanser had taken Father over to the stable to look at the horse and buggy, and since Mrs. Hanser was rattling on about all the delicacies Mother could make with pecans, I wandered over to the stable.

"Yes, she's a fine mare, Mr. Schmidt. No exaggeration."

I was surprised to discover Mr. Hanser could talk. In time I learned he could do this almost anytime his wife wasn't around.

"The missus is a mite inclined to exaggerate about the house, but I'm not about this mare."

"Yes, well, but as you were saying, about the house . . . ."

"I know. Needs some fixing. I suppose the hen house too if you're to raise some chickens. Raising chickens and doing a bit of farming should make a nice supplement to your income. See, sometimes the interest on the congregation's bonds and mortgages don't come to much. And that's what your pay's from. So a bit of farming can't hurt none. A frugal pastor can always make his way here. But about the house — tell you what, Mr. Schmidt, I'll personally take it up with the deacons. I'm sure we can set aside some funds to buy you some lumber. And I'll send my boy Simeon over to help you with the work."

"Thank you. I'd appreciate that. How many boys do you have?"

"Oh, about 22, I reckon. More than most folks around here."

"Twenty-two?"

"Oh, it's not all so many. Near Savannah some folks has upwards of 500." Mr. Hanser stopped to study Father's face. "Oh, I see what's puzzling you!" He laughed. "No, no, not sons. Boys. Negro slaves. Men slaves."

"Oh? Yes, well, if it's all the same to you I'd just as soon not use the services of a man in bondage. If it were people of the congregation . . . ."

"But Simeon's part of the congregation."

"You mean he's a member?"

"More than that. He *belongs* to the congregation. We all own him. I just take care of him. For the congregation."

"Mr. Hanser, if I can't have the services of free men, voluntarily rendered, I'd rather not have any."

Mrs. Hanser came over effusive with smiles. "Didn't I tell you, Mr. Schmidt? What do you say now? Oh, have I interrupted something grave?"

"Honey, Mr. Schmidt doesn't seem to approve of having bondsmen."

"Oh? Well, of course you don't, Mr. Schmidt. You're new here. But believe me, Mr. Schmidt, we can tell you a thing or two about slavery. In the beginning our forebears opposed it as much as anybody. More. But in time their eyes were opened to the good it does."

"Such as?"

"Why, it takes those poor, benighted souls away from heathenish Africa and brings them to this land where the Gospel shines so brightly. But you're a pastor. You should know *that!*"

"Yes, well, you mean you buy them for the sole purpose of evangelizing them?"

Her voice turned acid. "If we didn't work them, they'd laze away their lives with no way to support themselves. As for the evangelizing, that's what pastors are for, isn't it? Right now, Mr. Schmidt, you're only a foreigner with foreign ways. You weren't here when our forebears carved this fine home out of the wilderness. Everything's been done for you. So I'd suggest you apply yourself to adopting our ways and as soon as possible, or you'll find your stay among us, well, shall we say, less than pleasant?"

As soon as they had gone, Father put his arm around Mother and said, "Don't say it, Mamma, I know. It's not what you're used to."

"Not even a stove or a pump!"

"I know, I know. But we'll make out. Klaus and Hans can help, and if everything goes well, maybe by Christmas. . . ."

"In what century?"

Father tried to be cheerful. "But just think, Mamma, at least Hans hasn't run into any Indians."

"No, but if Maria runs into one of those spiders in the kitchen, it'll carry her off." Her body convulsed with what started to be a laugh but quickly turned to sobs.

4. Barefoot Soldiers

Father's nearest church was about a mile away. Though nothing like our finely-appointed sanctuary in Germany, it was respectable enough. So with the help of several members we spent the summer concentrating on the parsonage. We moved the furniture in, sold what we had no room for — like the piano — mended all that needed mending, and struggled to evict the former tenants who tenaciously clung to the place: ants, enormous spiders, roaches, ticks, and bedbugs.

In between chores and my staking out the surrounding piney woods for scenes of future battles, Father tutored Klaus and me in English, religion, history, and literature. In military science I tutored myself.

That fall Klaus and I were sent to a clapboard, one-room school about two miles away. To our misfortune, Mother dressed us in the grand style of the old country. My classmates took one look at our shiny, knee-length breeches, suspenders, white shirts and fluffy ties, and broke out laughing. "Get a load of the foreigners!" they hooted. The other boys wore long pants, coarse shirts with open collars, and no shoes at all.

Even the schoolmaster, Mr. Hildebrandt, didn't take kindly to our dress. "Son, you don't look like you'll make it," he told me. "But I'll make a man of you or break you trying."

My indiscretion during the second day of school didn't help endear me to Mr. Hildebrandt either. We had all taken our seats after the afternoon recess when Mr. Hildebrandt's great hulk darkened the doorframe. His close-set, beady eyes roved around the room. "I always said you all act like swine, but now . . . ." He sniffed the air as audibly as possible. "Now you even smell like swine! Might as well be in a barn as with the likes of you!"

He walked to the front of the room like a taskmaster inspecting slaves, then sat down at his desk. "I declare, you all smell worse here than from the door!"

Suddenly the older boys seemed unusually industrious. They busied themselves with their slates and books, keeping their heads down, though sneaking occasional glances at Mr. Hildebrandt.

He put a pot of coffee on the stove, which he kept burning even on the hottest days so as never to miss his thrice-

daily cup. Then he started rummaging through his desk.
He opened the bottom drawer and leaped to his feet.
"Horse manure! Who did it? Who filled this drawer
with manure?"
He paced up and down like a caged lion, waiting for an
answer.
Absolute silence! Well, almost. I giggled.
He stopped and glared. "Who's the hyena?" He must
have spotted my smirk. "You, Hans?"
"Sir?"
"So, the son of the new Lutheran preacher thinks it's
funny, huh? The abolitionist preacher's son! Well, when
I'm done with you, we'll see how funny you find it!"
He had me bend over while he applied 20 strokes with
a peach switch across that part of me which seemed peculiarly reserved for just such occasions. I didn't cry out or
shed a tear and thought this would help my standing with
the rest of the boys, but it didn't. To them I remained
a foreigner. Maybe they treated Klaus the same way, but
I felt only my own pain.
Many times during the next few weeks, until Mother
could make me clothes like the others wore, the boys
would say, "Hey there, Hans! My, but ain't you pretty,
though!" But the way they pronounced my name with their
nasal twang and slow drawl, it always came out "Hi-yands."
One day Ned, who turned out to be the strongest boy
my age, tried to put a blossom in my hair. "Your Mammy
forgot to dress you proper-like this morning," he explained.
That was the last straw. Forgetting what Father had
said about turning the other cheek, I buried a fist in his
stomach. He doubled up and fell back a few steps to re-
cover, his eyes wide open with surprise.
"Now, Hans, I means no offense, 'cause I ain't one for
fetching me no fight."
I figured I had him good and scared, so I rushed at him
with both fists flailing the air. Next thing I knew I lay

sprawled out on the ground with him standing over me. "I told you, Hans, I don't want no fight, so don't you go and drug one up."

I grabbed his legs and pulled him down, and we started wrestling. It wasn't much of a scrap, though. Maybe no one else was surprised, but I was astonished by the ease with which this boy, hardly bigger than I, had bested me. My nose was bleeding all over the place, my clothes were soiled and torn, and Ned wasn't the least bit hurt.

Oddly enough, from that time on the boys my age all respected me because Ned went around telling them what a great scrapper I was. In fact, he and I became the closest of pals, even though my mother didn't like him much. She had nothing special against him, just his unkempt appearance and the fact that he sniffed snuff. But Ned turned out to be a most loyal friend, and in spite of his physical agility and uncanny knowledge of nature, he always looked to me for leadership.

As for the older boys, they still looked down on me as I did on them. To me they were nothing but ungainly, barefoot farm boys who could never be soldiers. I even told Ned as much within their hearing.

Sam, the leader of the older boys, said, "You going to be a soldier, Hans?"

"Yes, but the lot of you," I sneered, "are fit only for the plow!"

"You? A soldier?" he laughed. "You ain't strong enough except to lift the church offering, preacher's kid!"

"And the only thing you all could lift is your feet in a retreat. You'd show an enemy no more than your hind sides."

"You oughtn't to said that, Hans," a second boy growled menacingly, "unless you're hankering for a fight."

"I don't want to fight you, Bob," I said, pointing at his left arm, which ended just below the elbow. He was born that way, I'm told.

"This?" he said, holding it up. "Don't you worry none about me. This won't improve your chances none. I can do anything you can. Now, c'mon and fight before I rip you to pieces."

He lunged at me and his fist caught me on the side of the head. He was considerably taller than I, so I stayed in close and whaled away at his belly. This kept his right hand from doing me any damage, but that stump of a left arm let go a cloudburst of blows on the top and side of my head. Before long we were both grappling on the ground, snarling and swinging and rolling. The fight lasted quite a while. I was hurt and my nose was bleeding all over him and me, but at last he cried, "Enough!"

"Hey, Hans," Sam drawled, "you're tough. Yes, sir, you've got scrap. How about coming with us 'uns Saturday morning for a hike?"

"What you about, Sam?" Bob objected.

"It's all right, Bob. Hans can take it. He's going to be a soldier boy some day. Right, Hans?" He turned and winked at the others.

I knew it was a trick of some sort, but I wiped the blood from my nose and said, "Sure, I'll go."

"Why don't you bullies leave him alone?"

I spun around to see who could possibly be speaking up for me. It was a golden-haired girl with big, blue eyes.

"Aw, if it ain't little Sally Jo!" Sam teased. "We ain't going to hurt Hans none, Sally Jo. How can we? He's going to be a soldier boy, I guess a real woman-charming soldier boy. Sure 'nough, a real woman-charmer, hey Sally Jo?"

She turned red and let out a "boo-hoo" heartrending enough possibly to draw even Mr. Hildebrandt away from a cup of coffee. Then off she dashed for home.

Saturday morning early I met the boys beside the old rice-stamping mill. Sam said, "We play soldier too, Hans. Saturdays we hike. Course, we ain't got us no fine shoes like you, but we 'uns'll try to keep up."

We hiked all morning along sandy roads, through corn fields and rice paddies, through briar patches and piney woods. We even waded chest deep across a brackish creek full of cypress trees. By noon I was dead tired and barely able to keep up, but the others were still as spry and nimble as wild hares, their bare feet apparently feeling no effects from the hike.

We stopped to eat in a stand of pines. The others broke out their lunch, but I hadn't brought any since I had not expected our hike to last this long. They sat there munching away, pretending they didn't notice my lack. With each mouthful, though, they licked their chops and commented on the tastiness of their tidbits.

"Hey, Bob, you sure should taste this here biscuit. Boy, is it good! Umm. How about a chaw on this sugar cane?"

"Never mind. I've got me some corn bread with butter and sorghum. You all ain't tasted nothing like this."

Sam sat down next to me. "Nothing like pecan pie, though," he observed with lip-smacking emphasis. "Nothing at all. Yep, like I always says, I'd risk anything for pecan pie. Anything!"

And so it went. I tried not to listen, but they got so close I could smell the food.

"Hey, Hans," one of them said, breathing his meal in my face, "ain't it a fine day for soldiering? But it sure does work up a body's appetite, now don't it?"

Finally Sam took pity on me. "Hey, Hans, you must be hungry."

"Me? No, not really."

"Well, I knows — good soldiers don't get hungry. But have some of my lunch anyhow."

"Really, I ain't hungry," I protested weakly.

"I knows, I knows. But humor me. I hates to go home with some of my lunch un-et. It's a sin to waste food, ain't that right? You know that, being as you're a preacher's kid and all. Help me out of sin, won't you, Hans?"

"Well, since you put it that way . . . ."

"I just knew I could count on you, Hans. Now, I don't need lots of help—just help with this here." He held up a grubby-looking bulb.

"What is it?" I asked.

"Kind of like a radish, only better. Take a taste."

In size and color it looked more like a cross between a radish and an onion.

"Come on, take a bite," Sam coaxed. "If you don't like it, you can just spit it out. Leastways I won't be sinning then, being as you tried it and all."

"You sure it's good?"

"Well, I'm not asking you to take my word, sacred as it is—only to try it for yourself. You'll see. Tastes something like a radish. Here." He handed it to me. "Take a big chomp."

They were all eyeing me, so I had to be brave. I bit into it. Yes, it did taste something like a radish—at first. The taste grew stronger, much stronger, too strong! I spit it out. "What is it?" I gasped.

"A jack-in-the-pulpit!" Sam shouted. The whole gang broke into uproarious laughter. "Growed in the woods by my house," Sam managed between laughs. "I dug it up for you myself."

My tongue reached the kindling point and burst into flames. My mouth turned into a volcano, my saliva into molten lava. I spewed the lava out. More formed. I didn't dare swallow lest it sear my throat and stomach.

I spit out some more, but the more I spit the more they laughed. So I quit spitting and just let the saliva overflow my mouth and chin.

After Sam recovered from his convulsions he said, "Now that Hans has et his lunch we can get on with the hike."

They set out single file, with Sam in the lead and me bringing up the rear. My shoes had dried stiff as boards from their soaking in the creek and began rubbing my feet raw. But this didn't bother me half as much as my mouth.

I was slobbering all over my shirt and pants. Every time one of the boys turned around and saw me he'd break into a broad grin.

On we trudged mile after mile with my mouth burning like a furnace every step of the way. Unlike a red pepper, the jack-in-the-pulpit wouldn't quit. Only my determination burned more fiercely.

"I'll see every one of them collapse before I will," I promised myself.

I began to manufacture saliva deliberately, hoping it would dilute the stuff corroding my mouth. This succeeded in getting my shirt sopping wet, and that's all. Meanwhile my feet began to rebel. I ordered them to keep moving, but they grew sluggish. I *demanded* that they keep moving, but by midafternoon they would have no more of it. My legs joined in the revolt and collapsed under me.

To my relief the other boys were out of sight. I propped myself up against a fallen pine and pulled off my shoes to examine the backs of my feet, each of which now had a large blister. I thought my tongue did too. I began licking it on my sleeve, hoping to wear off the flames. It did no good at all, so I went back to drooling helplessly.

Then I imagined how nice it would feel to be dead—no more burning tongue, no more blisters, none of those boys to face on Monday or any other day.

Suddenly Sam charged through the underbrush yelling, "Bang, bang! You're dead!"

From all sides my tormentors leaped out of the under-brush. "We caught us a soldier boy with his shoes off and his guard down," one of them jeered.

"C'mon, soldier boy," Sam said, "we're almost home. Just a mite piece up the road. Get your shoes on and we all can be moving on."

I wanted the earth to swallow me. It wouldn't, so I revived my pride, thrust out a drenched but defiant jaw and said, "I just stopped to remove a stone from my shoe. And

you didn't catch me off-guard. I knew you were there the whole time."

My words irritated Sam. "Is that so! Still think you're good enough to be a soldier, eh Hans? Well, we'll see." Fortunately the last part of the hike lasted no more than 15 minutes. By Sam's house I bid the group farewell. "Thank you for the hike," I drooled. "See you all Monday." "Hold on, soldier boy," Sam waved. "Stay a spell. We ain't done yet. Hiking's only part of soldiering. A soldier is got to shoot too."

He went into the house and returned with a long flint-lock musket. One of the boys set a pine cone on a fence post about 50 yards away while Sam loaded and primed the gun. When he had finished, he shoved the gun at me and said, "Hit the cone."

The gun was so long and heavy I could barely lift it, let alone aim it.

Sam yelled, "Don't be a-slobbering on the priming pan, you dunce! You get the powder wet and it won't shoot."

I spit out a mouthful of saliva, wiped off my chin, and tried again to aim the musket. With considerable difficulty I managed to get it pointed in the direction of the target. I pulled the trigger. The pan flashed, the muzzle blazed and roared and flew up in the air, while the stock kicked me in the shoulder and knocked me on my rump. My shot felled a tree limb that hung a dozen feet above and to the right of the cone. And the boys' laughter cut me to shreds.

Sam reloaded the gun, then ordered one of the boys to move the cone to a fence post 50 feet beyond the one I had shot at. He took quick aim and fired. The cone splattered into pieces.

I went home totally humiliated. A glass of milk healed my mouth, but what could heal my pride? Telling myself that I had something the others didn't — a soldier's courage — made me feel better, but not by much.

For the remainder of that school year the older boys kept on reminding me of the hike and shooting contest. So

I was relieved when school let out for the summer and I could get away from them for a while and perhaps come up with a way to get even.

5. The Savage

Mr. Mahlstedt, a member of the congregation, had presented us with a plump porker, but the creature had gotten loose in our yard, and now Father was providing us with no end of amusement. Trying to catch the pig, he looked so like a demented drunk that even Mother had to laugh.

"Honey," she called out, "what will you do with it if you catch it? You've never butchered anything!"

Father grunted, or maybe it was the pig, and again the chase among the pines was on.

Father didn't find the matter at all funny. He had scheduled a trip to Augusta and to Elberton in north Georgia, where he was to make contact with German-speaking Lutherans, but he didn't want to leave until this porker had been dealt with. At the rate he was going, the trip might have been postponed until Christmas, but Simeon, the congregation's "boy," came by and asked if he could help.

"Did Mr. Hanser send you?" Father panted.

"Oh, no, sir, Mr. Schmidt! I'm on a holiday."

"Well, butchering a pig is no way to spend it."

"But I wants to, Mr. Schmidt. It gives me pleasure to do something for a servant of the Lord. I'll have that old porker strung up and a-curing in a jiffy."

"But we don't have a place. . . ."

"Oh, I reckon as how Mr. Wilkins down the road'll let me use his smokehouse a bit! Don't you worry none about that."

Simeon was as good as his word. He completed the whole business with great dispatch, much to Father's relief.

That evening as Father lighted a cigar, he said, "Mamma, I think I'll take Hans to Elberton with me."

"But that'll cost. . . ."

"Yes, well, thanks to Simeon we won't have to pay for butchering the pig, and now that we have meat in store. . . ."

"What about Klaus?"

"We don't have money to take both boys, and Klaus has harvesting to do."

In a way Klaus had brought this on himself. My main chore had been to do the farming, his to fix the chicken-house and raise chickens. But he had tricked me into trading jobs, and while as yet I had no chickens to raise, he now was stuck reaping what he had sown.

"Besides," Father continued, "if Hans is ever to be a pastor, he has to find out what it's like."

"Father . . ." I began to argue.

"I know, Hans, you want to be a soldier. But you're young yet. Someday you may change your mind. If you do, I want you to have the right education. Besides, you'll enjoy this. We'll be heading into old Indian country. Of course, Indians used to live around here too, but they had a great nation in north Georgia until just 20 years ago."

"Are some still there?"

"No need to fret. They're all gone now."

"I wasn't fretting, Father."

"No, of course not. I forgot. You're the Baron's great, great grandson."

We took the train up to Augusta, and during our stay there we saw blue-clad soldiers at the Federal arsenal. Their uniforms weren't as smart as Prussian soldiers wore, but I decided that if I couldn't return to Germany I could always be an American soldier.

On the last day of our stay the heavens opened, and the deluge didn't let up until we boarded our train for Washington, Georgia.

Washington was at the end of the railroad spur, so there we had to rent a team of horses and wagon from the local livery stable. At noon we set out for Elberton, about 30 miles away. We should have known better.

The sun had been out for several hours, but the red clay road was still miry, causing horses and wagon much labor. Three times that afternoon the wagon bogged down almost axle deep in the mud. Once we spent more than an hour finding enough branches and rocks to give the wheels traction. By sunset we were probably little more than half way to Elberton.

"Well," Father told me, "we could keep going, but at this rate it might take all night. Or we could let the road dry out while we camp here for the night."

The latter seemed more adventurous, so I leaped at it.

The dense forest pressed in so closely on both sides of the road that we were forced to make the road our camp. Father gathered pine needles to make some mattresses, and I gathered firewood. Afterwards, as he started cooking supper, he said, "Hans, see if you can find some big branches — you know, the kind with several hours' burning in them. We'll need enough to last the night."

Without an ax, thick branches short enough to be useful were hard to come by among the young pines. So I searched further from camp — around the bend at the top of the hill and down in the hollow where I saw some oaks and giant Georgia pines. But down there tangles of vines carpeted the ground beside the road. So I wandered into the woods a little. Twenty feet into the woods I found a nice, thick branch I could drag along, then another. Why hadn't I done this before, I wondered. It wasn't that I was afraid of the woods. Absurd idea! Maybe Sam and the other boys surpassed me in hiking, but in courage I was miles out front! But it *was* getting dark. I had to get back before Father started to worry.

"*Father* worry!" I heard Sam mock. "Who's kidding who?" My mind pictured him standing in my way, his yellow teeth sticking out of his freckle-spattered face. "What do *you* know, Sam?" I said quite loud. You'd never go this far into a darkened wood all by yourself." I quickened my pace. "It's just that I got to get back. My father *does* worry — a whole lot!"

I was almost back to the road when the thing I dreaded most happened. An Indian stood in the road looking at me! I screamed and turned and sped back into the woods. The Indian shouted at me. I tripped over a vine but was up in an instant, screaming and scampering deeper into the woods. Again I tripped and again I bounded up and off.

"Hans!" I heard Father call. "What is it?"

I plunged through the heavy undergrowth and up the hill in the direction of our camp. The Indian came crashing through the brush behind me. Again I tripped over a vine and fell to the ground. I tried to get up but my feet were tied in knots.

"Hans!" Father called again, quite close now. I struggled to untangle my feet. Then I felt his hand on my head.

"Father!" I cried. "It was an. . . ." I rolled over and looked up. "INDIAN!"

I tried to scream again but my vocal cords were playing dead. The Indian said something that I couldn't understand. He stroked my head, then pulled me to my feet.

"Hans!" Father yelled as he burst into sight. He stopped in his tracks to size up the situation. The Indian immediately said something in a strange language, and I pulled away from him and ran to Father.

The Indian tried talking to Father, only this time he gestured with his hands. Apparently Father thought he was friendly, so he motioned him to come eat with us. But I wasn't taken in as Father was. I mean, I wouldn't have screamed or run from a *friendly* Indian.

As Father finished preparing supper, the Indian brought more wood for the fire. My eyes remained fixed the whole time on his shirttail, which I just knew concealed a scalping knife.

During supper I pretended I didn't suspect a thing. Above all, I had to keep Father from thinking I was afraid. He kept trying to communicate with the Indian, and at last told me, "I think he's a Cherokee from the mountains in Carolina." He went on to tell me about the great Cherokee nation in northern Georgia, about how civilized it was, how the Cherokees built houses, farmed the land, invented an alphabet, ran their own newspapers and had even a capital and an ambassador in Washington, D. C. But when gold was discovered on their land, Georgia insisted that the Federal Government expel them.

"Did the Federal Government?" I asked.

"Oh, yes! In spite of old peace treaties. Made them go to Oklahoma, but some escaped to the mountains in North Carolina."

The Indian started writing in the mud.

"See, he must be a Cherokee!" Father said.

The Indian spotted the Bible lying on top of Father's pine-needle mattress. He pointed to it and started talking excitedly, then opened his shirt and showed us the cross he wore around his neck.

Father said, "The Moravians have done a lot of missionary work among them. I'd guess he's one of their converts. But I can't figure out what he's doing here in Georgia. Anyway, he wants to be a friend."

The Indian accepted Father's gestured invitation to spend the night with us.

I relaxed somewhat when I saw the Indian pray before going to sleep. Still, my suspicion that he planned to murder us in our sleep, then steal the wagon and horses, would not relax. I had heard many stories about how treacherous and thieving Indians were. So I slept with one eye open, at least for an hour or so.

By the time the sun woke me, the Indian had a fire going and was preparing breakfast. Seeing that I was awake, he came over and said something to me. I didn't understand the words, but his tone and eyes were so kindly that I got the message. I realized now he was no savage.

"Good morning," I said.

Proud that I was no longer afraid, I tried to conjure up Sam's lean figure so he could see my lack of fear. At last I had him, standing by the wagon shaking with fright to the tip of his upturned toes and drawling, "Oh, Hans, how can you be so brave?"

"Coffee brewing?" Father asked, shattering my fantasy.

I looked up. He was brushing the pine needles off his shirt while the Indian still busied himself with breakfast.

Bam!

The loud explosion almost sent me clean out of my skin. Father jumped up. The Indian lay on the ground, his arms and legs flailing the earth. As he rolled over in a violent twitch, I saw blood all over his head and face. His arms and legs stiffened for a moment and quivered. Then his whole body relaxed, and he lay stretched out on the ground.

Father ran over to examine him. "He's dead!" he gasped.

"Course he's dead!" someone called out from behind me. I spun around and saw a man with a musket walk into view. "When I shoots me an Injun," the man continued, "he's dead."

"You shot him? But why?" Father demanded.

For a time the man didn't answer. He just poured some powder from his horn into the gun's muzzle, stuffed in a wad and ball, and started ramming them in with the rod.

"Why?" Father demanded louder than before.

"Why?" the man replied with a careless shrug. "He's a Injun, ain't he?" He gave the Indian a light kick to make sure he was dead, then looked up and asked, "Got a cup of coffee for a stranger?"

Father's voice shook with emotion. "You can drink coffee with his blood all over the ground?"

The man sat down and calmly replaced the percussion cap on his musket. "He weren't nothing but a savage," he answered in a puzzled tone, as if amazed that we couldn't comprehend the force of his logic. "Nothing but a savage!"

That had been my impression too. That's what I had always heard at school both here and in Germany. But now as I eyed this man helping himself to a cup of coffee beside the Indian's body I began to wonder just who were the *real* American savages.

6. Beautiful, Beautiful Blue Eyes

My pal Ned introduced me to a new setting for our mock battles, but reluctantly because his heart was in the river and the seas. More than anything else he wanted to be a sailor, or more exactly, a pirate. He often told me about the pirates who used to put in at Savannah and bury their treasures on the coastal islands, and several times he tried to entice me to go rafting with him on the Savannah River. But Father had forbidden me, and my experience with the sea being what it was, I decided to obey the commandment about honoring parents.

So instead of playing pirate Ned was forced to play soldier, and he brought to it a vast knowledge of the area. Over at the Ebenezer steamboat landing by Jerusalem Church he told me, "You know, during the Revolution British soldiers used that there church for a stable."

"You mean British soldiers were here where my Father preaches sometimes?"

"Thicker than skeeters in August." He pointed at the weather vane atop the squat steeple. "See the fish up there? Was a swan once. When I was just a young 'un. Had a round shot plumb through it. By a Redcoat."

"You saw it with your own eyes?"

"Yup."

Nearby he showed me an old log house perforated with holes. "The British shot it up with a cannon," he told me as he kneeled down to pull a tick off Tag, his faithful hound. "But old Nat Greene and Anthony Wayne gave 'em what for. Sent them Redcoats a-scampering clear back to England."

"Who's Nat Greene and Anthony Wayne?" I asked.

"Who's they? Why, they's the best generals what ever lived." He sniffed a pinch of snuff. "Well, excepting for the Baron, of course."

So now I had some new heroes, also an authentic site hallowed by battle to play on. And how I looked forward to those Sundays when it came Father's turn to preach at Jerusalem Church!

It was one of those Sundays in late September at the afternoon catechetical service. I was sitting in the front row, imagining that the church was Wayne's headquarters and that General Wayne was poring over maps spread out on the pew.

"This is the road we'll march by, men. We attack Savannah in the morning. Hans, your regiment will lead the assault."

I looked up from the map, proud to be given this assignment. But what met my eyes sent maps, Wayne, and headquarters dissolving into the mists of the past. In the choir stall directly in front of me sat Sally Jo.

She sat profile, with her cute little nose looking straight ahead at the base of the pulpit. Someone beside her was reciting a portion of the catechism, but her head didn't turn to listen. I wanted to get her attention, so I knocked my hymnal on the floor. She looked straight ahead. Someone else started to recite. Her eyes didn't deviate even an inch from the pulpit.

All of a sudden I wished I had eaten dinner, but earlier I had been too excited about going to Jerusalem Church. Now I had this feeling in my stomach. It was going to rumble, I just knew. I pressed in on it. It squealed. Sally Jo's eyes remained fixed. I bloated it out. It gurgled.

"Stephen, can you recite the meaning of the Second Article?" Father intoned from the pulpit. Whoever Stephen was, he sat there like a dunce in utter silence.

"Recite, Stephen!" I cried inwardly. "Recite LOUD!" More silence.

Then came the roar. My stomach roared and squealed and gurgled and roared some more. And that clown Stephen just sat there! Well, I got Sally Jo's attention, all right. She looked at me, broke a slight smile, then turned back to her preoccupation with the pulpit.

After the service the adults stood on the church lawn talking about Abraham Lincoln, the Republican candidate for president, but I paid little attention to them. My eyes were filled with Sally Jo.

Ever since school had reopened she had entranced me. Somehow last year I had hardly noticed her, either at church or at school, but now — wow! That golden hair. Those deep-blue eyes, and the shy way she tilted her head. I wanted to talk to her, but all I dared do was sneak a glance at her now and then.

At supper that evening I couldn't eat much.

"Are you feeling ill?" Mother asked.

"Mamma, I think Hans is in love," Father announced.

"I am not!" I shouted. "I don't care two snaps for Sally Jo!"

Oh, what an idiotic blunder! Now they all knew. Klaus too.

"Mamma," he tattled, "Hans didn't pray before."

"I did too!" I said, greatly relieved that he hadn't noticed my slip about Sally Jo.

"Well, I didn't hear you!" he argued.

"Well, I wasn't praying to *you!*"

At school the next day my heart started pounding and my face flushed everytime Mr. Hildebrandt called Sally Jo's name. I felt sure everyone noticed, but no one said anything. All week long I couldn't muster up the courage to speak to her except in my daydreams. But on Friday Mr. Hildebrandt called Sally Jo up before the class.

"Now, face the class!" he ordered in his most tyrannical manner. "And you explain just why you didn't finish your history lesson!"

Suddenly her tear-dikes burst, flooding those big, blue eyes, while her slender body shook with sobs.

The boys all snickered, and I wanted to demolish them, especially Sam, and Mr. Hildebrandt too.

During recess the boys again made fun of her. "Hi, crybaby!" Sam teased.

Even Ned joined in. I gritted my teeth but didn't say anything.

After school they started teasing her again. Bob, the one-armed boy, knocked the books out of her hand and said, "You going to cry again, big baby?"

She did! And the boys ran away and left her.

When they were out of sight, I picked up the books and waited for her to start walking. Then I walked beside her. All the way to her house we didn't say a word to each other—just "Good-bye" as I turned toward home.

That weekend Sally Jo and I talked up a storm in my daydreams. Maybe it was good practice, because during recess Monday I spoke to her.

"I'll walk you home after school."

She tilted her head in that shy manner. "All right, Hans."

It wasn't much, but she had said my name!

After school Ned asked me if I wanted to go 'coon hunting with him and Tag. I said no and he allowed as how he'd play the Baron or General Wayne if I preferred, but I told him I had to do chores. So he went off with Klaus and the other boys, and I ran down to where the road forked off to Sally Jo's house. When she came by, I silently joined her. Maybe it wasn't the same as walking her *all* the way home, but this way the other boys didn't know.

I did this all week long, and Ned grumbled about my having to do more chores than he even though he had a "whole passel of young 'uns at home."

Sally Jo and I never said much. I didn't know what to say, and she was so shy. But she talked with those big, blue eyes. I couldn't look into them for more than a few seconds though, because then I'd blush and she'd blush and we'd both hang our heads as we continued on our way.

I made up my mind on Friday to show her how I felt, so I could study her reaction and see if she felt the same about me. I figured this is what the Baron would have done — set up sort of an intelligence-gathering mission.

Saturday I carved her and my initials on a great gnarled oak that stood in the center of one of my very private battlefields. Monday I planned to take her past that tree, pretending that we had stumbled onto it quite by accident.

During recess Monday I told her, "I know a shortcut to your house. Would you like to see it?"

Her head tilted. "All right, Hans."

After school and after the now oft-repeated excuse to Ned, I led Sally Jo onto the "shortcut" to her house. We cut through the woods behind the schoolhouse, skirted a small lake, and waded through some heavy brush to the small clearing dominated by the great oak. My heart started to pound just thinking about the tree. The closer we drew the harder it pounded.

As we broke through the underbrush beyond which stood the tree, I heard Tag bark. Then the older boys spotted us. Ned and Klaus were with them. They started hooting and laughing.

"Look who's walking the crybaby home!" Klaus jeered. My mind worked furiously to find an excuse, but Sam had already discovered the tree.

"Hey, and look at what's carved on this here tree! H. S. LOVES S. J. K.!"

"They're not my initials!" I yelled.

"C'mon, Hans, I reckon you're not sneaking off home with her through the woods either. Sally Jo's a-walking all by herself." Then he began in the most awful singsongy voice, "Hans is in love with the crybaby!"

All except Ned took up the chant. He just stood there dazed, as if everything he knew about me were a lie and I were not the great, great grandson of the Baron after all. The others continued the chant: "Hans is in love with the crybaby!"

"I am not!" I protested. My courage was now in shambles. I couldn't ignore what the others thought, or follow what I felt in my own heart. So I yelled, "She's nothing but a crybaby!" I knocked the books out of her hand and changed the chant to "Sally Jo is a crybaby! Sally Jo is a crybaby!"

In that instant before she started to cry her eyes widened with a look so unbelieving, so hurt, that my stomach turned to lead, and I sped away like a wounded stag.

7. Gator Country

The following week I worked feverishly to catch up on my chores—hauling water from the well, fixing the chicken-house, feeding the rooster, hen, drake, and duck we had finally purchased. Then I went over to make amends to Ned.

I suggested we spend Saturday playing pirate and rafting on the river.

He sneezed, sniffed some snuff, sneezed again, then decided he could overlook the matter of Sally Jo.

Early Saturday he took me some miles down river from Ebenezer landing to see Stephen Gaulke, whose father supervised a "wooding up" station for riverboats. Stephen already had a raft built, and once I learned that he was not the clown who couldn't recite the Second Article during that catechetical service, I decided I liked him a lot.

We could have had a perfect day except for Klaus. He had discovered our plans and said if we didn't take him along, he'd tell Father.

Klaus took his shoes off and went down to inspect the raft. Ned seized the occasion to fetch two relatively fresh cow pies from a nearby pasture and dump them into Klaus's shoes.

Not to be outdone, I struck upon another idea.

"Let's give Klaus a good scare. He can't swim, so when we're down the river a ways, let's tell him we can't control the raft. We can make him think the current'll sweep us out to sea."

Ned and Stephen went for the idea. Even Tag's plumed tail wagged its approval. So when we found Klaus at the water's edge inspecting the raft, we invited him to climb aboard.

For more than an hour we drifted down the Savannah in search of pirate's treasure, with Stephen steering the raft by means of a broad oar. On both sides of the river moss-draped branches and tangled vines drooped down to the surface, obliterating the shore line. The mud-colored waterway wound between these walls of green, widening now and then to admit the waters of some creek or to by-pass a placid pocket of green slime and swamp grass in which basked some alligators.

As we drifted around a large bend, the river suddenly widened and the comforting walls of trees receded from the banks, unveiling broad stretches of almost treeless marshes. Except for a few herons, the whole scene was so desolate that an eerie feeling gripped me.

"Hey, we're caught in the current!" Stephen yelled. Tag barked and my heart leaped, but a quick glance at Stephen reassured me. He winked. "I can't steer the raft!"

Klaus grew pale. "What does that mean?" he asked nervously.

"What does that mean? It means we all'll be carried plumb out into the Atlantic and never be seen again!" Ned informed him.

"Oh," said Klaus trying to reassure himself, "we'd have to go by Savannah first! Folks there'd be bound to see us and send out a boat to catch us."

"No!" Stephen argued. "The current is stronger on the back river. It'll carry us clear round the far side of Hutchinsons Island. Nary a soul in Savannah'll see us."

"We'll be lost at sea!" I chimed in. "We'll drown!"

For some minutes Klaus sat quietly contemplating his fate. Then, as we rounded another bend, he spotted a large, marshy island in the middle of the river. "Steer for that island!" he shouted.

"I can't," Stephen answered. "The current's powerfully strong. It'll carry us plumb past the hind side of the island."

"Let me try," Klaus said as he grabbed for the oar.

Stephen resisted and tried to argue. "Get back, or you'll knock us into the water."

The two of them struggled for control of the oar. Ned and I tried to pull Klaus away, and Tag added to the confusion by jumping on us and barking. But the more we struggled, the more Klaus panicked. The raft went out of control, going into a lazy spin and drifting first this way, then that.

"Let Stephen steer it!" I yelled. "He knows how! It's all a joke!"

But Klaus wasn't listening. In the struggle he nearly knocked Ned overboard.

"Stop it, Klaus!" Ned pleaded, backing up his plea with a kick in the shins, but Klaus struggled all the harder. I was trying to get ahold of Klaus's hair when Stephen lost his grip on the oar. I watched with alarm as it drifted away. Ned lunged for it, but it was already beyond reach. Then, *whump!* We hit the island. I lost my balance and fell into the water. Ned and Stephen tumbled in too. Klaus scrambled ashore and, as near as I can figure out, in his panic kicked the raft with his foot.

Ned came to see if I was all right. The water was only two feet deep where I fell in, so I was all right except for being soaking wet. But by the time we had all collected our wits, to our horror we saw the raft drifting away down river.

Ned and I started after it but could make no progress because the oozie river bottom held our feet like a vise, and where we stood the water was too shallow for anyone but Tag to swim in.

"Now you've done it!" I yelled at Klaus.

"Done what?"

"Well now, if that don't plumb beat all!" Stephen exclaimed. "We're stranded on this here island and you ask 'what?' "

"Well, whose fault is it you can't steer?" Klaus retorted.

"Stephen was doing fine 'til you interfered," I told Klaus.

"Doing fine? We were headed for the Atlantic!"

"Oh, Klaus, we was just joshing!" Stephen explained. "I was steering it before you botched things up."

"Joshing? You was joshing?" Klaus looked at Ned and me to confirm what Stephen had said.

We nodded. "Just a joke, Klaus."

For a minute Klaus tried to digest this bit of news. Then

he said with a sneer, "Some joke! Well, funny men, what now?"

We looked around the island. A lone, scrubby tree stood a third of the way down the right side of the island — maybe 200 yards away. It was probably the only part of the island not covered with at least several inches of water. Where we stood the water came half way to my knees.

"Klaus, why couldn't you have stayed home and practiced your violin?" I asked. "Now we're in a real mess." Turning to Stephen, I added, "You're lucky you don't have a brother. Sometimes I wonder why God had to make older brothers."

"You better wonder about gators too," Ned said. "This here is gator country."

I could swim, but not far enough to reach either shore, and Klaus couldn't swim at all. So we were stuck but good.

Ned told us to set out for that lone tree. He might as well have told me to swim the river, because my feet sank into the muck up to my shoe tops. To get them out again was like pulling molasses taffy. And since the swamp grass stood two feet taller than I did, I could no longer see the tree, let alone be sure that I would ever reach it. But I plowed ahead.

"Look out!" Ned cried.

My feet stopped mid-stride. "What is it?" I called back.

"Didn't you see it?"

"No. What?"

"A gator, just a few wiggles to your right."

My hair stood on end. "I don't see it," I fairly screamed. "Where?"

"Well, I saw it for sure, ain't been but a few seconds ago. It's gone now, but keep your eyes peeled."

I didn't need to be told that.

"Maybe I was just a-seeing things," he added.

Anyhow, I edged to the left with almost inhuman effort, keeping my eyes sweeping back and forth through the grass to the right. I tugged on the grass so I could plow ahead faster. It cut my hands, but I wanted to reach that tree! Desperately!

"Where is that gator? Maybe lying in wait for me up ahead. Maybe I'd better pray. No. I've disobeyed Father. Well, but if I first asked God to forgive me . . . ."

And that's what I did—rushed off a quick prayer for pardon and, with that preliminary done, started bombarding His throne with prayers about that gator. Make that gator go away. Better yet, make it be on the other side of the island right now. Best still, make it never have existed.

Through the grass I could now see the top of the tree. We were getting close. Almost there. Another few dozen steps or so and we'd be away from that thing I had prayed out of existence.

I looked over my shoulder, back toward where Ned thought he saw it.

Ouch! I stumbled over something and lost my balance. It moved. I heard a sucking sound. My blood curdled. "The gator!" I screamed, but still heard its hissing, threatening snarl.

I spun away, but the mud held my feet, pitching me face-forward into the grass. I screamed again, but all I could hear was its enraged roar and its powerful jaws snapping at me. I screamed again and tugged at the grass with all my might. I wiggled desperately to get away and let out another scream, only to have it drowned out by the gator's thrashing and snarling.

Then I heard Klaus scream. No, it wasn't a scream. It was a . . . a . . . I don't know!

The "gator's" jaws closed on my shoulder. I kicked over and swung and hit its . . . . No. I hit Ned in the arm. *Ned* had me by the shoulder!

"Hans, you gone mad?"

"The gator, Ned, the gator!"

"No, Hans! Look." He shook me again.

And again I heard Klaus, but he wasn't screaming. He was screeching with laughter. "Hans thought it was a gator!"

"See," said Ned, "it's just a log what got washed up here. Nothing to be a-feared of."

I looked back and saw a log, just a dumb, old log!

"Well, brave warrior," Klaus mocked, "see how still it lies in death. You've just slain your first log! Or have there been others?"

I pulled myself up, wiped off some mud, and said, "Ha, you fell for it, Klaus! Did you really think I thought that old log was an alligator? Ha, I was just trying to scare you, smarty!"

"Oh, sure you were!"

"Ask Ned. He knows. I was just pretending. Right, Ned?"

"C'mon, Klaus, move your feet and quit flapping your jowls," Ned ordered, "or a no-pretend gator'll be along before we reach that there tree!"

Like I said, Ned was a loyal friend.

When we reached the tree, Stephen started breaking off twigs and small branches.

"What are you doing?" Klaus asked.

"I've got a flint and iron. We'll make us a fire here to signal the next steamboat what passes."

"But we don't have any money for passage," Klaus pointed out.

"I'll explain things to the captain," Stephen replied.

We waited by the tree almost two hours. Then suddenly beyond the swamp grass on the far end of the island we saw it, looking like a great white, smoke-belching swan as it came around the bend and headed up river.

"Light the fire!" Ned called. Here she comes!"

When the boat stopped and the gangplank swung out to us, we climbed aboard, to be greeted by a number of curious people, including the captain.

"You boys are a bit far from home. I trust your parents know," he said. My heart sank.

"No," Stephen answered, "but I can explain."

"I suppose you'll explain you have no money for fare either."

"Yes, sir, that's true enough, but if you'll let me explain . . . ."

"Never mind," said the captain. "I know your daddy and I know you, Stephen. You're not the kind to get in such a fix." He turned to Klaus and his face grew stern. "These three aren't old enough to know better, but you! Come with me. You're the one that's got the explaining to do — leading youngsters astray!"

Stephen, Ned, and I watched as the captain led Klaus by the ear up to the pilot house.

"Boy, I sure wouldn't want to be in his shoes," said Stephen.

Suddenly we all remembered Klaus's shoes and giggled. "In them on no account!" Ned laughed. "Say, Hans, it's kind of lucky Klaus came along, don't you think?"

I didn't answer, but I did come within a whisker of thanking God for older brothers.

8. Ten Tin Soldiers

On Christmas children are supposed to be surprised by the presents they get. I didn't want to be. I wanted a set of tin soldiers, nothing else, and I made every effort to let Father and Mother know that this is what they should get me.

I spotted them on a shelf in a Savannah store — 10 tin soldiers and a toy cannon. The soldiers wore blue great coats, red tunics, and white breeches, just like the soldiers of Prussia in the days of Frederick the Great and of the Baron.

I pointed the set out to Father.

His brow wrinkled. "Yes, well, I suppose they'd be nice, but they're pretty expensive. Perhaps you see something else you'd like."

"No, Father, just that set of soldiers."

For the next weeks I talked about nothing else. Even Sally Jo and my search for a way to get back at Sam took a back seat in my heart to those tin soldiers. Klaus talked constantly about the new violin he wanted, and little Maria about the doll with the hoopskirted satin dress and crinoline petticoat.

Each passing day only heightened my excitement. I couldn't begin to count the plans I had for those soldiers. They were my idols. They represented almost everything I wanted and everything I hoped to be.

At last the day arrived. The Christmas Eve service was beautiful enough, but I got a case of the wiggles when Father launched into his sermon. I kept wishing he would finish it so we could get home and open our presents.

Eventually the service ended, but Father wouldn't be rushed. He had to wish each person down to babies-in-arms a blessed Christmas.

After an interminable delay we arrived home and followed our custom of gathering about the Christmas tree and singing a few carols. Father offered a prayer thanking God for sending His Son. I had nothing against giving thanks but kept wondering why it couldn't have waited until after the presents.

The instant the prayer ended I snatched my present and started tearing off the wrapping. Why did they always waste time wrapping the presents? Now I couldn't remember: Did the soldiers have gold buttons on their tunics or not? Stupid box! Stuck! Ah, there—it's opening. More wrapping! That's more like it. Here they come. I see color. Yes, the beautiful color of their . . . .

I stood in stunned silence, unable to believe my eyes. Marbles! Nothing but a box of stupid marbles! I pulled all the paper from the box. There must be more! Underneath maybe. I emptied the marbles onto the rug, then examined the box again. Nothing more. Maybe another present under the tree. No, Klaus was unwrapping his and Maria hers. No other presents in sight. Father and Mother were eyeing me closely. I didn't want them to see my disappointment, so I reached up and with head bowed gave each of them a hug. I even tried to force a thank-you. I don't think I managed it. My eyes were misting up, so I raced out of the parlor and into my bedroom.

It wasn't long before Klaus entered. He was crying too, though quite softly. Then from the parlor I heard loud crying. It was Maria. What a Christmas!

Klaus didn't get a new violin, just some wax for his old one, and rosin for the bow. Maria got a little rag doll Mother had made, not the nice one we had seen in the Savannah store.

Klaus, Maria, and I spent one miserably sullen Christmas. I just knew Father had done this to me deliberately, because he didn't want me to be a soldier.

We took our seats around the table for our Christmas dinner. No one said a word, but I could see that Maria's eyes were still red. So were Klaus's. Mother fidgeted a moment with Maria's braids. Then Father bowed his head and began a prayer I'll never forget:

"Father in heaven, forgive me; I have sinned. In my heart I complained. I faulted You for the little interest the congregation received on its mortgages and bonds this year. I faulted You for the little money they could pay us. Dear God, You know what gifts I wanted to give our children and the stove I wanted to get Mamma, and I blamed You because we couldn't afford these.

"Forgive me, Father—I forgot. I forgot the pain You must have felt that Christmas when You saw Your Child Jesus going without the glories of heaven so He could lie in a poor manger for us. Make me grateful, O Father, that You have given us the best gift of all—Your Son, and that You have given us also one another. We are rich indeed."

After the prayer he didn't look up, but I saw the tear stains on his cheeks. How miserable I felt then! What an ungrateful wretch I had been! I had thought only of my own disappointment, never dreaming of how disappointed Father felt because he couldn't afford to give me those tin soldiers, or Klaus his violin, or Maria the new doll, or Mother the stove.

After dinner I gave him and Mother a big hug. "Thank you for the marbles," I said, and I meant it. I still felt disappointed over not getting the soldiers, but at least now I understood.

9. Fugitive Slaves

I was grateful to Mr. Hildebrandt. Knowing how we loved holidays, he gave us an extra one by coming down with an attack of the gout.

This gave Ned an idea. Originally he had set out to catch some skunks for their pelts, but he so enjoyed our holiday that he decided to place his first catch under the schoolhouse, which stood several feet off the ground. He calculated that by throwing a few stones at the skunk he would render the schoolhouse unfit for classes for at least two extra days. But so far, no skunk.

It was getting dark as he and I returned from checking the traps.

"Maybe Mr. Hildebrandt won't notice the smell," I told him. "Sam's feet have gotten him pretty used to strong smells."

"Yeah. They're enough to make a buzzard puke," Ned laughed. Suddenly he stopped and motioned up the road toward a group of slaves headed our way.

"Oh! Oh!" he whispered. "We're in for it."

"Why?" I asked.

"Count them. They's eight of them. The law allows no more than six to walk the road together. They must be runaways. And we's seen them."

"What'll we do?"

"Too late to git. They'd catch us. We better just walk on by like we didn't notice."

I started to tremble. The closer we drew, the bigger they grew until they were giants who could stomp on me like an ant. I wished I were an ant and could burrow into the sand. As we drew even with them, I could see they were eyeing us carefully, especially Tag who walked at Ned's heels without a sound.

"Evening, Masters," one of them hailed.

"Evening," I croaked, the word sticking to my tonsils. My legs itched to run, but I made them walk until we rounded the bend. Then Ned and I slipped into the pines and executed a retreat far swifter than any we had ever practiced.

At my house we found Father sitting on the porch. I motioned wildly but was too breathless to talk. "What is it, Hans?" he said, trying to shake it out of me. Bit by bit Ned and I gasped out what we had seen.

"Did they chase after you?"

"We was too . . . busy a-running . . . to look," Ned got out, "but I . . . don't think so."

"Well, then, we've got nothing to worry about. Wish them Godspeed."

Father sat back and calmly puffed on his cigar. His manner was so reassuring that before long Ned and I forgot the whole business and began to pretend we were lying in wait for some Redcoats walking unsuspectingly toward the front gate. The ambush worked beautifully. We slaughtered two whole regiments of Redcoats and left their bodies piled higher than the rail fence before we felt sated and Ned went home.

I had just sat down on the porch with Father when we heard a lot of clucking coming from the chickenhouse. "That fox again," Father whispered. He fetched his rifle from above the parlor fireplace and signaled me to follow him.

We took up our position behind the pecan tree which outflanked the chickenhouse door and gave us a good field of fire. The commotion inside the chickenhouse continued.

"The door's open!" Father scolded as softly as he could. "I told you to make sure it was kept shut."

I thought I had shut it, but what could I say?

The door creaked, then swung open wide.

"That's no fox," Father whispered.

Footsteps were coming right toward us. Father stepped out from behind the tree. "Stop!" he commanded.

A large slave came to an abrupt halt only a foot from the muzzle of Father's gun. From each of his hands dangled a chicken.

"Don't shoot me, Master!" he cried.

"Then you put those chickens right back!"

"Yes, Master, right away!" And faster than he had taken them he put them back, with Father following close behind to make sure.

"Why were you stealing our chickens?" Father wanted to know.

"I was hungry, Master."

"Hungry? Doesn't your master feed you?" The slave

made no reply. "Who's your master?" Again no reply. Then we heard faintly but distinctly the baying of hounds. The slave's eyes flashed in the direction of the sound. "They're after *you*?" Father asked.

"Please, Master, don't let them catch this poor nigger," he pleaded.

Father lowered his rifle. "Get in the kitchen," he motioned.

I felt terribly sorry for the slave when I saw him in the light. His pants were torn, his bare back bore the scars of a whip, and his feet were bleeding.

Father fetched a small ham that hung down in the well, filled a canteen with water, and began wrapping some bread and cheese in a kerchief when Mother walked into the kitchen. For a moment she just stood there studying the slave. Then turning to Father she said, "What are you doing, Father?"

"Feeding a hungry man."

"You mean you're helping a runaway. Aren't you?"

"Mamma, you've seen the slave market, and slaves being auctioned off like cattle, and children separated from their mothers, and wives from their husbands. You've seen them beaten. Can you ask me to send this man back to that?"

"But if they catch you, you'll go to prison," she protested.

The baying of the hounds was much louder now, and the slave began to fidget. "Please, Master," he begged.

Father went to the door and listened. "They're coming through the back woods." He handed the food to the slave and said, "Hurry out and around the house. Cut through the woods on the other side of the road!"

"Thank you, Master. God bless you, Master." The slave dashed off into the darkness, and we hurried into the house.

Mother started in again on Father. "They'll put you in prison for this."

"What's so disgraceful about prison, Mamma, if you're sent there for helping a fellow human being? You know, Jesus was sent to prison."

"But what about the children? And me? I can't bear the thought . . . ."

A loud confusion of clucking and barking interrupted her. Moments later there was a knock at the back door. She sank down onto the sofa as Klaus rushed from the bedroom to see if we knew what all the racket was about. Father hushed him, then went to answer the door, taking as much time as he dared.

It was Sheriff Braun, a member of our congregation. "Evening, Mr. Schmidt. Hate to break in on you this way, but we've tracked some runaways to your house here."

"Runaways?" Klaus asked.

"Runaways. I'm sorry but we've got to search."

Without waiting for permission he pushed his way past Father and Klaus. He searched the bedrooms and parlor, then went out to the kitchen. We followed him, and, to my horror, I spotted blood stains on the kitchen floor. I held my breath for fear Sheriff Braun would see them. His eyes shifted from Father to Mother, then to me and Klaus, then back to Father.

"They're not here, are they, Mr. Schmidt?"

"No, not that I know of."

"You're sure of that?"

"Yes," Father said thoughtfully. "I'd be very much surprised if you were to find them around our house. Would you like to look in the store room? And maybe the stable and chickenhouse?"

"Hmmm." The sheriff rubbed his chin as he lowered his eyes. "Not here, you say?" He paused. "But they have been."

We all remained silent.

"See?" he said, pointing to the blood stains on the floor. He waited for some sort of explanation, then continued, "Mr. Schmidt, you didn't help the runaways, did you?"

"No," I answered for Father.

"Hans!" Father said, giving me a reproachful look.

"Yes, I helped one."

Klaus gasped. "You did?"

"You know the law, Mr. Schmidt," said the sheriff.

"Yes, well, it's a bad law that protects slavery," Father answered.

"A bad law? The Bible itself supports slavery."

"Any slavery the Bible allowed was of a different kind. It did what our prisons are supposed to do today—take care of criminals and prisoners of war. But these Negroes aren't criminals. They were stolen from their land and forced to come here."

"That may be," the sheriff interrupted, "but they're here now. And some master paid a good price for them. So they're his property. Aren't we supposed to help our neighbor hang on to his property?"

"Not if it's *stolen* property. Besides, if you want to use Old Testament laws to defend slavery, then follow those laws. They command that every 50 years all foreign slaves be set free. Well, 50 years is passed—several times over. So you might say I was only helping a man get what was long overdue him."

"Then why do all the other pastors preach in favor of slavery? Even the Catholic bishop in Savannah and the Episcopal bishop of Georgia do. They all say it's a good way to bring the Gospel to the Africans."

"By enslaving them? Is that how Jesus worked? Or by love?"

"Well, lots of white folks love their slaves, just like their own!"

"Like their own what? Cattle? House? Dog? If they'd follow the Bible and love them as *themselves* . . . ."

"Mr. Schmidt, I can't argue with you on Bible matters,

but you see the spot you put me in. I . . . ."

One of the deputies burst into the kitchen. "Sheriff," he cried, "we just spotted a slave making a break through the woods."

"Where?"

"On the other side of the road!"

"That far? Hmmm. Well, then let him go. I'm more interested in taking the man who helped him."

"Someone helped a runaway?" the deputy asked. "Who would do such a thing?"

"We'll have no problem catching the culprit." Sheriff Braun turned to Father. "Right, Mr. Schmidt?" He turned back to the deputy and said, "Well, don't just stand there. Go arrest him!"

"Who?" the deputy stammered.

"Who? Must I do everything for you? Place the culprit in your arms? Blockhead! Head up toward Springfield and look!" Then doffing his hat to us he said, "Night, all. Oh, and, Mr. Schmidt, that was a fine sermon Sunday! Meant to tell you earlier."

We stood there speechless as the sheriff and his deputies disappeared into the night.

The next morning Mr. and Mrs. Hanser stopped by on their way to church.

"Just had to stop a minute," Mrs. Hanser said. "Did you all hear about the slave uprising last night. No, of course, you couldn't have. Well, some runaways from north of Springfield headed down toward Savannah, and just across the Chatham County line, not far from that Methodist Church — you all remember, the one I told you about? Well, anyway, the runaways burned down a house with a man and his wife and two young 'uns inside. Isn't that just terrible? And after the way folks fed and clothed them slaves!"

"Mrs. Hanser," Father interrupted, "how do you know the slaves did it?"

"How do I know? Well, how do you suppose the fire got started? All by itself? Oh, they did it all right! But a patrol from Springfield caught them not three miles away. And did they teach them darkies a lesson! Covered them with pitch and set them afire, every last one of them!"

"You must be joking!" said Father, recoiling at the news.

"It's true, I promise!"

"O God!" he exclaimed. "Taught them a lesson, you say? Some lesson! Around here anyone who gives slaves a lesson in reading or writing gets fined or jailed. But *this* lesson is allowed! No trial, just kill them. Yes, that's a lesson — in lawlessness and violence! But what's going to happen when the slaves learn that lesson?"

"Well," she said, "that's a sorry attitude for a white man to have!" She spun around and stalked out the door.

10. When Abe Entered the White House

It was a day I'll never forget. Ned met me on the way to school with the news that he had caught two skunks. We hardly had time to work out the details of his plan when events at school quickly canceled everything.

A black wreath hung on the door. Inside, black bunting draped the entire classroom. Everyone milled about, curious as to what all this meant.

We took our seats without a word as Mr. Hildebrandt entered, looking more the monster than usual. "No doubt you all are wondering who died," he said. "Today I am in mourning for the United States. I trust that none of you taxed your brains reading the paper or noting that today Abraham Lincoln moves into the White House."

I had not read the newspaper but knew that Mr. Lincoln's election to the presidency last November had ignited war-like rallies in Savannah and elsewhere.

"Some people call him *Honest* Abe." Mr. Hildebrandt began bellowing like a lion with a bone in its throat. "*I* call him *Black* Abe. That atheist has singlehanded killed the Union. When he was elected president, we knew what it meant: that he'd be sending those Yankee hypocrites down here directly. You know why? To take our slaves from us. And why are those Yankees *hypocrites?*" His eyes blazed as they roved from student to student. "You don't know?" he roared. "Then I'll tell you! They say we *mistreat* our slaves. But have you ever seen a slave without food or clothes or shelter, or without a doctor when he's down with the fever? No! But just visit a factory in Yankee country! You'll see whole families of Poles and Irish and Italians working from sunup to sundown, and with what the Yankees pay them they can scarce feed or clothe themselves, let alone fetch a doctor when they ail. That's the kind of hypocrites Mr. Lincoln wants to set on us!

"Well, you all know that several weeks ago Georgia withdrew from the Union and joined up with six other states to form a confederacy. Lots of folks hereabouts weren't in favor of our leaving the Union. But now it's done and we all had better get behind our state and defend her."

He lifted the coffee pot slowly from the stove. By this time I had learned his habits well enough to know he was backing up for a charge. Then it came. "You all know what Mr. Lincoln is going to do now?" Again his eyes blazed as he searched the classroom for someone to answer. "Hans!" he barked when his eyes met mine.

"No, sir," I stammered.

"Then you'd better wake up, boy, and learn! He's going to send soldiers down here to *force* us back into the Union. You mark my words! He's already butchered the Union, but he won't let it lie. He's going to try to resurrect its dismembered corpse! By war!"

Mr. Hildebrandt spooned some sugar into his coffee, then twisted his lips and said, "From now on you older boys will spend recess drilling. Down in Savannah they're drilling in Forsyth Park—the Republican Blues, the Chatham Artillery, the German Volunteers, the Oglethorpe Light Infantry. They're all getting ready." He banged the spoon on his desk. "And I want *you* to be ready too! Hear?" Looking over at my section of the classroom, he added, "You younger boys won't need to drill. When Lincoln's soldiers come, we'll finish with them before you all can contribute to our victory."

During recess we watched Mr. Hildebrandt drill the older boys in marching. How we envied them! After school, not to be outdone, we picked up lengths of split logs from the wood pile, put them over our shoulders, and marched home.

As we approached my house we broke into a wild charge, yelling and hooting and shooting our "guns."

I was still shooting as I entered the parlor. "Hans!" Father called out. "I'm trying to write a sermon!"

"We're going to war, Father. I was just practicing."

He emerged from his bedroom. "Where did you hear that?"

"Mr. Hildebrandt told us. Isn't it exciting? There *is* going to be a war, isn't there?"

He planted both hands on my shoulders and looked at me earnestly. "Maybe, Hans, but real war isn't like the way you play it. Real war means real killing. Can you understand that? Fathers get killed, sometimes mothers and children too. People's houses get burned down. And many people starve or die of disease. I know you think it's all a game. But believe me, you'd be much better off praying that war doesn't come."

Sometimes fathers make no sense at all. This was one of those times. Sure, I knew some people might get hurt. But then, there was the rest of it—parades and uniforms, bands playing and girls waving. And maybe I'd get to be a soldier. What excitement and adventure, and all those gallant heroes and dashing deeds and shining victories! These were the things Father didn't understand. For once I felt I was infinitely smarter than he.

I changed my clothes, fed the chickens and ducks, then raced barefoot down the sandy road.

From among the spindly pines came the sound of slaves singing as they repaired one of their huts. The hammers pounded in rhythm to the words: "Go down, Moses, to Egypt land." They seemed to strike with greatest force at the words: "Let my people go!" I didn't know then what the words meant. I thought they were simply the story of Moses and Pharaoh in Egypt, not a prayer for a modern-day Moses to deliver these people from bondage.

Up the road my friends were marching. "Hey, Hans," Ned called, "don't we look right smart? We Georgians can lick the whole United States!"

I joined their ranks, and so did Johnny, an 8-year-old black boy who often waited for us after school. As we got in step, I added to the boast: "We Georgians can lick the whole world!"

Toward dark our army broke up for supper. I waved good-bye and set off for home with Johnny tagging along. He and I were still soldiering it with every step we took. I could feel the saber whisking my leg, and the cartridge box strapped to my side. My march was proud and erect as my rifle moved rhythmically to the cadence I barked: "One, two, three, four. One, two . . . ." Then I saw him leaning against a tree, his teeth protruding from his wretched grin like two ranks of gilded organ pipes. Sam!

"Well, if it ain't the little pantywaist preacher's kid still playing at soldier! And he brung along his 'boy' to do the fighting for him."

I wanted to belt him, but I knew what he'd do to me, so I resorted to words instead. "Ha! Georgia's joke factory! What amusement you'll give the Yankees!"

His grin vanished.

I went on. "You out practicing up on running, Sam? Better get back at it. The Yankees'll be here soon enough."

"You hush your mouth, Hans. One thing I don't cotton to is anyone saying I'm yellow. So you mind what you say or I'll forget how dang little you are."

As suddenly as it had vanished his grin returned. "Say, I hope you don't take no offense to what I said and go shooting me with that there gun of yours. I notice you got your finger on the trigger. Is it a-getting itchy?"

My face reddened as I pulled my finger from the knothole. "This ain't no gun. It's just a piece of wood I was carrying home for the stove."

His grin slithered clear around his ears. I flung the "gun" from my hand and walked away, but from behind me he barked out the cadence: "One, two, three, four! One, two, three, four!" I struggled furiously to get my feet out of step. Then he laughed and yelled, "Go home, little soldier! Georgia'll take girls in her army before she'll take you!"

That ended my soldiering for the day, but it set off a spark in my strategic brain. Sam had humiliated me once too often. Now he would feel the wrath of the Baron's great, great grandson!

11. Sweet Smell of Revenge

That Ned had caught two skunks instead of one made my strategy almost foolproof, but I still had a few tactical details to work out.

It would have been easy to design a plan that would have kept Sam from ever knowing that I was responsible. But I *wanted* him to know. Yet I had to do it in such a way that he'd have only himself to blame. Then he'd have no call to get back at me.

So the problem was how to bait Sam into trapping himself. Even this I had partly solved. His pride in his own bravery would make him rise to the bait, but what could I use for bait?

Week after week I observed Sam's every move at school — his habits in the classroom, the way he marched his knobby knees at recess, the way he gorged his face at lunch, what he talked about, even the way his grin poked fun at me. Meanwhile Ned and I fed the skunks, pulling the cages by means of long ropes over to the food we had placed for them.

It was early April when the last piece of my plan fell into place. The older boys were sitting off by themselves near the woodpile, eating their lunch and looking condescendingly at us younger boys.

Bob, the one-armed boy, bit into a piece of pie. Sam's eyes grew wide. "Hey, Bob, is that there pecan pie?"

"Yup," Bob replied with his mouth full.

"Boy, what I wouldn't do for a bite of that there pie!"

"Yup!"

"I mean, I'd risk anything for a piece of pecan pie, like I always says."

"Yup."

"You heard me say that lots of times, hey, Bob?"

"Umpf." Bob started stuffing it down faster.

"Well, you don't have to be a pig about it! I wish just once my mother'd make me one, like Granny does when she comes a-visiting."

"Yup," said Bob, sucking the last of the pie from his fingers.

"You're a swine, Bob. You knows that, don't you?"

"Yup."

"Yup! Yup! Some pal you are, knowing that I'd do anything for a piece of pecan pie! I told you often enough!"

Well, there it was, and so obvious too! Why hadn't I thought of it before? Sam was right. He had said that before, lots of times, and everyone in the school had heard him at one time or another.

Now all I needed was Mother's cooperation, but that took some doing. For several days I coaxed, begged, and pleaded for her to make me a pecan pie.

"A whole pie just for yourself?" she asked. "What on earth for?"

I assured her I planned to share it, but still I couldn't get her to say yes, even though I volunteered to do the shelling. So I proceeded to do her little favors, like cleaning out the chickenhouse without fussing, and even things she hadn't asked me to do.

After I plugged up a few knotholes in the parlor floor, she said, "Hans, you can be so sweet—when you want something." Later she went out to the storeroom and got out a bag of pecans. I helped her shell them, and in no time at all she had baked the biggest, juiciest bait I had ever seen.

That night I lay in bed carefully rehearsing my lines.

When you're going to school, Fridays always seem beautiful. This particular Friday dawned with special glory, and it wasn't simply the silky spring air that did it. I was a bit nervous—so many things could go wrong, but the prospects so excited me that I walked with a spring in my steps and a song in my heart.

"What's the matter with you?" Klaus wanted to know. I ignored his question and clutched the paper bag which held the bait more tightly. He glanced at it and growled, "You'd better share that pie like you said or I'll tell Mother."

"Don't worry. I don't plan to eat it all. Only one piece at most."

Lessons that morning barely limped along. At morning recess I studied Sam. He paraded with the air of a conquering hero.

When lessons resumed, I counted the ticks of the clock on the back wall. I looked out the window and

searched each passing cloud for familiar shapes. I stuffed
a dead cockroach down through a crack in the floor, and
even tried drawing pictures of Mr. Hildebrandt. But that
was too gruesome, so I switched to studying Sally Jo's
turned-up nose, and dimples, and the way her golden hair
twisted around her ear.

Again I looked at the clock. Almost noon! My heart
started pounding like a drummer on a binge. What if I said
the wrong thing? What if Sam skipped lunch and went off
with the gang? He did that now and then.

"Class dismissed!" Mr. Hildebrandt announced. I picked
up my large bag and met Ned at the doorway.

"I'll need your help after school today. All right?"

"Sure, Hans. You mean today's the day?"

"Tomorrow too, I think."

Outside we found Sam and his pals sitting in their usual
place over by the woodpile. I led Ned and some other boys
over near the woodpile. We sat down on the grass facing
Sam and spread out our lunch. Sally Jo and several other
girls sat on the doorsteps, and the older girls sat under an
oak nearby. This was good, because Sam liked to show off
in front of them.

I carefully removed the pie from the bag and set it
out in plain sight. Sam hadn't started talking yet; he was
too busy devouring a biscuit. I scooped out one of the eight
wedges and set it on top of the rest of the pie so that when
Sam looked up he'd be sure to know what kind of pie this
was.

He raised a chicken leg to his mouth but stopped half
way, his mouth gaping and his eyes bulging at my pie.

"Hey, fellas, get a load of little Hans and that there
big pie!" Suddenly he waxed charming. "That pecan,
Hans?"

"Yes."

"That's a powerful big pie. Need some help with it?"

"Some. I sure can't eat it all."

"I'll help you, Hans. Like I always says, I'd do anything for pecan pie."

That's what I had been waiting for! "Talk, Sam! That's all you are is talk!" A deathly silence fell over the school-yard.

His eyes narrowed. "What you mean by that?"

"Just that. You always talk about how brave you are and what you'll do if the Yankees ever come down this way, but that's all we've heard — talk. We've all heard it, especially the girls. You really make sure they hear you."

An undercurrent of "oohs" swept through the yard. Sam grew red and his hands formed fists.

I had backed him into a corner with no way out other than by flying into me, so I quickly changed tactics. "You want the pie, Sam?"

He scowled as he looked around at all the spectators, but if he had been on the brink of charging into me, my offer made him hesitate.

I was so scared I would have gladly handed him the pie and ended the incident, but I caught Sally Jo watching me, so I went ahead but with greater care.

"Maybe it isn't all talk. Maybe you're as brave as you make out, only you ain't had a chance to prove it. If only you had the chance, then we all 'd know."

The swelling in his knuckles seemed to go down. "What you want, Hans? That I should fetch Mr. Lincoln's soldiers and bring 'em down here so as I can prove something to you?"

"Well, no, you can't do that. But what about all that other talk you make? Like about pecan pie. This pie." I held it up. "Would you really risk anything for it? Like you always say?"

He looked around. Every eye was on him. "What you getting at?" he asked suspiciously.

"I mean, if that ain't all just talk, if you'd really be willing to risk anything, you can have this pie."

"Well now, you don't expect me to risk my life for some pie!"

"No, not life. Or limb. But how do we know you'd risk anything at all?"

"'Cause I says so!"

"Well, maybe we all would believe you," I said with a sweeping gesture toward the onlookers, "if we saw you just once risk something—anything—like for this pie."

"Hans," he asked with growing irritation, "what you got in mind?"

"Well, meet me at my father's church tomorrow morning, at, say, 9 o'clock and you can prove to us all just how brave you are. I'll give you a chance to risk something, like they do in war, the prize for victory being this here pie."

He eyed me with great suspicion, so I added, "Just a small risk, one that won't even hurt you. It won't take nearly as much bravery as tangling with Yankee soldiers. What do you say, Sam? We'd all like to know if you're really brave." I turned to Ned and the other younger boys. "Wouldn't we?" I asked them.

"Yeah!" they replied in chorus, with a few female voices thrown in.

Sam looked about to study his pals and especially the older girls. "For the pie?" he asked. I nodded. "Nine o'clock you say?" Again I nodded. He threw back his head, then announced, "I'll be there, Hans, but you better bring that there pie!"

Hooked! A stroke of genius that even the Baron would have admired!

During the afternoon recess, while Sam was out drilling —with a little less swagger than usual, I thought—I made sure all the younger boys would be over at the church in the morning. Ned asked the girls if they were coming. After school he told me, "Everyone, and I means everyone, is a-planning to come."

Perfect. Without a good audience Sam might still back down.

After school and again after supper Ned and I set things up. It wasn't easy dragging the skunks all the way over to the church. Opening their cages to let them escape into the outhouses was a ticklish affair, but by dark we had everything ready for the morning.

The day dawned, to quote the hymn, "bright and beautiful." Father and Mother were curious about my behavior, but for once Klaus didn't blab, since he was as interested as the others in seeing the showdown.

Ned, Tag, and Johnny, the little Negro boy, met us at the church. Klaus kept asking where the pie was, but I told him simply that this would be revealed in due time.

Gradually the crowd gathered. The younger boys first, then the girls, including Sally Jo. And last came Sam leading the procession of older boys. I could almost smell success.

When everyone gathered around, I addressed Sam: "You said you'd risk anything for pecan pie, just like you'd risk anything for Georgia."

"Not life or limb for pecan pie!" Sam corrected.

"Right. But what we all want to know is, will you really risk life and limb if war comes? I've set up here a small test of your bravery. It's something like soldiers have to face."

"How so?"

"Well, in war you win a lot or you lose a lot. But you don't win *and* lose. That's the risk you take, right?"

"So?"

"So if you're brave, you run the risk. If you win, you're a hero. If you lose, well, you're dead."

"What's that got to do with the pecan pie?" Sam demanded.

"We want to see if you'll really run a risk to win the pie — like you always said you would."

Sam glanced around at the gathering. "Yeah, but in war you knows what the risk is. What's the risk for the pie?"

I motioned everyone to follow me around back. To the left of the church stood an outhouse marked "Gentlemen." To the right stood a second marked "Ladies." "You see those two outhouses?" I asked.

"I'm not blind," Sam growled.

"Well, in one of them there's a shelf. On it sets a paper bag with the great victory prize — a whole pecan pie. Eight wedges."

"You sure know how to build up a body's appetite, don't you? And what's the risk?" His freckles swelled with suspicion.

"Just pick one of the outhouses. Go give it a couple hard thumps on the door, then charge in like a brave soldier attacking Yankees. If you pick the right one, you're the winner, and you'll see the pecan pie on the shelf — the spoils of victory."

"And if I picks the wrong one?"

"Then you don't get the pie. And like a loser you won't be too happy about what happens to you."

"And what might that be?" he demanded.

"Nothing as bad as if you lost as a soldier. You won't be happy, but at least you won't get hurt."

"No!" Sam objected. "I don't run no risks 'til I knows what the risk is."

Ned started the younger boys going. "Ain't scared, are you, Sam?"

"Big, brave Sam, ha!"

Even the older girls started working him over.

Sam turned defensive. "But even soldiers know what the risk is. I'm entitled to know that much!" He aimed his remark at the girls.

I made a quick decision. If I told him the exact nature of the risk, he'd have no comeback afterwards. And if he

backed down, the humiliation he'd suffer would be success
enough for me.

"All right," I announced, "I'll tell Sam the risk. In the
wrong outhouse is a skunk. He won't bite or claw, so you
see how small a risk Sam's taking."

A big hee-haw swept through the group.

"Small risk!" he exclaimed. "What about my clothes?"
One of the older girls yelled, "Them rags? C'mon now,
Sam! They're a walking compost pile!"

He looked around for a sympathetic face but found not
one in the whole crowd, not even among his pals, who were
chuckling over the prospects. I suppose they felt like
winners either way: the fun of watching Sam skunked or
the thrill of maybe sharing a wedge of the spoils.

The younger boys and the girls began taunting Sam.
"I didn't say I wouldn't do it!" he protested. He gave
me a glare that filled me with satisfaction. Then he scolded
his pals, "I don't see none of you volunteering. There's
not a ounce of bravery in the whole lot of you, but if you
all came to see bravery, you all 'll see it!"

He studied the gentlemen's outhouse, then swung around
to study the ladies'. "Fine place to put a pie!" he muttered.
At last he reached his decision. He set out quite smartly for
the gentlemen's, but the closer he drew the slower he
walked.

I clamped a hand over my mouth, and when Sam swung
around right by the door, Ned repeated, "Don't forget,
Sam! Three nice hard thumps on the door, then go a-charg-
ing in!"

"I knows," Sam called back in a whisper, as if afraid
to disturb what might lurk inside.

He stood there trying to work up his nerve. In fact he
took so much time that the girls started riding him. That
did it. He pounded on the door.

I convulsed with silent laughter. He pounded on it again,
then again. He opened the door a few inches as if getting

ready to charge in, then suddenly slammed it shut and beat a retreat.

"Pfew! Was a skunk, sure 'nough," he said sheepishly.

"You didn't follow the rules!" I shouted. "You're supposed to go charging in there!" The others agreed.

"Well, Hans," he whined, "besides being brave, soldiers has got to be smart. Even the bravest soldier knows that when a skunk starts a-going off, it's a time to git."

"But that weren't the rule!" Ned objected.

"So who made the rule? Hans? So who's he? I ran the risk, which proves I'm brave. I just outsmarted the skunk, so I'm the victor!"

Though the girls seemed unimpressed by his reasoning, the older boys cheered him. This emboldened him all the more. He threw out his chest in his show-off manner and crowed, "As the victor I now claims the spoils, namely, that there pecan pie." With that he headed for the ladies' outhouse.

I ran over to block his path. "You can't!" I shouted. "The rules said you could pick just one, and you made your pick."

"Out of my way, sonny boy," he said, pushing me aside.

"But that's cheating!" I objected. Sally Jo shouted her agreement.

Sam stopped. "Oh, I forgot to tell you, Hans! When I said I'd do *anything* for pecan pie, I meant some cheating too!"

I was in a real fix and had to come up with something quickly. In my desperation I protested absurdly, "But that's a *ladies'* outhouse! Maybe someone's in there!"

Sam stopped before the door and made a deep bow in my direction. "You may be right, Hans. Let's see." He gave the door three hard kicks and called, "Any ladies in there? No? Then here I comes!"

He grinned a victorious grin at me, pulled open the door, and waltzed right in.

"Yee-aah!" he screeched, nearly stepping on the frightened skunk! "Yee-aah!" he screeched again as the skunk darted between his legs and fled.

The crowd exploded with laughter while Sam stood there fairly dripping with skunk oil and stinking to high heaven. He flung himself on the grass and rolled over and over while we all withdrew to a respectable distance.

"Lookit him!" Ned laughed. "Groveling about like a lame hound dog in a meat house!"

My nostrils picked up the sweet smell of revenge as Ned banged me on the back in congratulations. Sam tore off his shirt, and I figured it was time for me to tear off for home.

From behind me I could hear Sam yell, "Hans, you cheated!"

I yelled back, "So did you!"

Things hadn't gone off cleanly. Sam now knew I had planted a skunk in both outhouses, so he had cause to get back at me. Yet that yelp when he saw the skunk and that look on his face fortified me against whatever he might do to me later.

As I fetched the pie from the store room and set it on the kitchen table, Klaus told Mother what had happened. She shook her head but couldn't help laughing. Unfortunately Father overheard the whole thing and asked sternly, "Where did you say all this took place? In the *church* outhouses?"

Suddenly I heard Sam. I ran to the storeroom window and looked out. He stood in the middle of the road, shirtless and screaming at the top of his lungs, "Come out, Hans! I wants you! Hear?"

Father went out and called back, "Some other time, Sam. Right now he's mine!"

Father paddled me good, but I kept thinking of the look on Sam's face and laughed louder with each spank. So Father finally gave up and went into the house. And unless my ears were playing tricks, he was in there slapping his knees and laughing.

12. Then Came War

It was April 16 — my 13th birthday — and Sam didn't
show up for school. If he had been plotting to get back
at me, events moved too fast for him.

The day before, Fort Sumter had fallen, and we received
news that President Lincoln had called for volunteers to
force our Confederate States back into the Union. This
meant war. In response many young Georgians rushed off
to enlist in our army. Sam and several of his pals were
among the very first, enlisting in a fife and drum corps.

After school Mother tried hard to keep me and my friends
entertained at my birthday party, but it wasn't much of a
party without Father. At breakfast he had seemed distant
and mysterious, as if some dark secret were troubling him.
Now he ignored us and sat inside the parlor, talking to
several men of the congregation.

I opened the front door to invite him to join us in the
games but hesitated to interrupt the conversation.

"Fort Sumter is on South Carolina territory," one man
was saying, "so I reckon South Carolina had every right
to seize it from the Federals, the same as when Georgia
seized Fort Pulaski back in January."

"That's so," a second replied, "but *firing* on the fort
was a mistake. It's given Lincoln just the excuse he needed
to make war on us."

There was a pause in the conversation, so I spoke up.
"Father, did you want to join in the games?"

"Later, Hans. I'm busy right now."

His refusal was polite enough but apparently was meant
with more finality than his words indicated. The afternoon
wore away and my friends went home, and Father never
did come out to join us. One of his callers went home, but
the other, Mr. Mahlstedt, stayed for supper.

During the meal I tried to hide my hurt feelings. It
wasn't necessary; Father barely ever looked up from his
food or spoke a word.

Immediately after devotions he and Mr. Mahlstedt adjourned to the house; so I parked myself on the porch and pouted. I did not mean to eavesdrop, but the front door was open and their conversation was again about the war — obviously an exciting subject to the great great grandson of the Baron, though I did think they were carrying it a bit far. I mean, why should a war be allowed to spoil my birthday?

I heard Mr. Mahlstedt say, "I'm joining up."

"You?" Father asked with surprise. "Fighting to defend slavery?"

"No, Mr. Schmidt, you know better than that. I've never owned a slave or believed in slavery. And many of the men being recruited have never owned slaves either. This is a fight for our homes, for our families, for Georgia. Slavery isn't the real issue; it's independence for our state."

"I don't see it that way," Father replied. "I know you and others like you mean well. But the issue *is* slavery. No one talked of secession or independence or of a Confederacy until the slave issue arose. All the other issues — tariff, states' rights, you name it — they're all connected to slavery like spokes to a hub."

Just then I coughed.

"Is that you, Hans?" Father called out.

"Yes, sir."

"All right." After a pause he called again. "Hans, would you please close the door?"

I shut the door and pouted more than ever.

Some time later the door swung open and Mr. Mahlstedt stepped out. He turned in the doorway and said, "Well, good night, Mr. Schmidt. Thank you for the meal and for listening. And God guide you in your decision. By the way, what does your wife think?"

"Shh!" Father answered. "I haven't discussed it with the family. I'll tell them after I've decided."

Hadn't told us what? So he does have a secret! Throughout the remainder of the week I speculated as to what it might be. Go back to Germany, maybe. Or move to Canada! It'd be just like him to do that to me, now that I'd have a chance soon to be a soldier, and in an honest-to-goodness war!

Sunday at the end of the morning service Father motioned the congregation to be seated.

"The service next Sunday," he announced, "will be at 3 o'clock in the evening. Reverend Mr. Dorow will conduct it. The week after, when Mr. Dorow is due to preach at his other churches, Reverend Mr. Koenig of Savannah will conduct the service."

I looked at Mother to see why he had said that. She seemed absolutely bewildered.

"You see," he continued, "I won't be able to conduct services here for a while."

He started unbuttoning his black robe. Then with a single sweep he opened it wide, revealing a navy-blue coat with gold buttons, and light blue trousers with a broad gold stripe on each side.

"Next Friday I report to the First Infantry Regiment, Georgia Volunteers, at Pensacola, Florida," he said. "I am now a chaplain in the army of the Confederate States of America."

His announcement created quite a stir at church, but at home afterwards it was like a funeral parlor. Mother moved about the kitchen speaking to no one and looking at no one. I hung the kettle over the fire for her and Klaus set the table, but following her cue, we said nothing, even though I was bubbling over with excitement and pride.

The silence was so contagious that even Maria caught it, and we ate dinner without a word. Once Father dropped his fork on his plate, but Mother didn't even look up. Only when he opened the Bible for devotions did she finally speak up, but without lifting her eyes from the table. Her voice nearly broke.

"That was a nice way to let me know!"

"No," Father answered. "It was cruel. But it was the only way I could keep you from trying to change my mind — a trick I read about another pastor doing back during the Revolution."

"But you . . ." she said with considerable emotion, "you who have always disapproved of slavery!"

"Mamma, I'm not doing this for slavery. Thousands of boys are going off to war. They need a pastor as much as people at home, maybe more. And many of them have never owned a slave."

She broke into tears. "And many of them have!"

He reached over and put his arm around her. "And that makes them sinners — like the rest of us. Didn't Christ come to save us all, including slave owners? Isn't the Gospel for them too?"

Maybe Mother didn't understand, but I was happy as a louse in a chickenhouse. At school the next day I made sure everyone knew that my father was a soldier, like I was going to be.

Thursday at the Central of Georgia railroad station in Savannah Father shook my hand the way he did with grown-ups. "Keep up with your home lessons in Greek," he told me. "You may need that some day if you decide to become a pastor. Try to spend as much time on Greek as you do on history. And write me about your progress. Oh, and take care of your mother — like a good soldier!"

He gave Mother and Maria a final kiss, then disappeared into the crowded train. Tears flooded my eyes. Somehow I had never dreamed that war would be like this, that it would take my father away from me.

His train pulled out promptly at three, but by that time I had already made up my mind to join him.

13. They Also Serve

My increased chores kept me from laying serious plans
to join Father. Besides school and my home studies in that
wretched Greek, I now had more than a hundred chickens
and ducks to care for, and the rooster wouldn't sleep nights
unless I personally carried him to his roost.

Still, I was doing some training. Having talked Klaus
into chopping the firewood and hauling the water in trade
for my taking care of the mare, I had a chance each night
to mount the mare and practice being a cavalry officer.

With the war, Mother's chores increased too. Almost
every day she and the other women met at church to knit
socks or plan a farewell for departing soldiers or to pray
for victory. Some of the ladies even made plans to evan-
gelize their slaves. I guess they wanted to make sure
God understood the advantages of slavery and would be
on our side.

By the time school let out for the summer Arkansas,
Tennessee, and even North Carolina had joined the Con-
federacy. But news of the fighting in Missouri and western
Virginia wasn't too good. When we heard about the fighting
in Virginia, Mother started to worry because in May
Father had been transferred to the 7th Georgia Infantry
Regiment and sent to Virginia.

One day Ned and I were over at the Ebenezer landing. He
showed me how his riverboats and river obstructions would
guard the river, and I was showing him where I would
position my landward defenses.

"Shucks," he said, "why'd they take Sam and his ilk and
leave a general like you and a sea dog like me behind? We
can fight good as them."

"Even better," I answered, "but we're too young."

"I heard a bunch of boys from a military school over
in Carolina is going to the fight. And they is only a year
older than us 'uns. They is going to be a fife and drum

corps. Even the navy takes young 'uns like us for powder monkeys if their folks says it's all right."

"Really?"

"Yeah. But my father'd never give me no permission."

"So, who needs permission?"

Right then and there we decided that he, Tag, and I would run away to join the fighting. We'd go home and smuggle our fathers' rifles and ammunition, some food and blankets. Then after dark he'd sneak over to my house, where I'd be hiding in the stable hayloft. By morning we'd be across the river by the Savannah-Charleston railroad bridge and could hop a freight heading north toward Virginia.

When I got home, Mother and Maria were over at the church and Klaus was out planting. So I had no trouble getting Father's ammunition. But since the absence of his rifle from above the fireplace would be too conspicious, I let that go till later.

By the time Mother came home, I had some bacon and cheese hanging down in the well.

"Why are you staying in the kitchen on such a nice day?" she asked after a while.

"Oh, it's too hot out, and Ned has chores!"

Later I got some parched corn and beans from the storeroom and hid them in the hayloft, but I still needed some bread and utensils. So I continued hanging around the kitchen.

Mother grew increasingly curious. "Hans, it isn't like you to just sit in the kitchen. What's the matter?"

"I thought I saw a mouse in there," I told her, pointing to the storeroom. That was a tactical blunder, because she immediately started searching the storeroom and I had to give up trying to get the bread and utensils until after supper.

It was almost dark by the time I had all the supplies rolled up in a blanket and stashed in the stable. I had even managed to put a dead snake in Klaus's bed, but I still had to get the rifle.

Klaus was sitting on the porch with Maria and Mother, who had just finished the supper dishes. So I sneaked through the back door, grabbed the rifle, and hurried out again. When the others went inside, I raced across to the stable, climbed up into the loft, and waited.

"Sure, Mother will be angry," I told myself, "but Father will be proud. And when the war's over and she sees me covered with medals, she'll be proud too. So will Sally Jo. She may even cry when she learns about my wounds."

I heard Mother call out the back door: "Hans! Time for bed!" The door shut again.

It was already dark but no sign of Ned. I lay back on the hay and waited and worried. Someone was bound to notice Father's rifle missing if Ned didn't get here soon.

Mother came out and called me louder than before.

Where was that Ned anyway? I grew impatient, but what could I do? So I waited some more. I waited and scratched and waited, and Mother called me once again.

What was keeping Ned? He should have been here an hour ago. I climbed down to peek outside. It was almost black as pitch now.

Suddenly I heard a bloodcurdling scream. It was Klaus. Apparently he had found my going-away present in his bed, but too soon—I hadn't gotten away yet!

I was just climbing back into the loft when I heard Klaus somewhere near the chickenhouse tattling to Mother: "Mamma, that son of yours put *this* in my bed!"

"He did more than that. He took your father's gun," she told him. "Did he say anything to you about running away?"

"No. He didn't have cause to run away till now! Oh, when I get my hands on that brother!"

"I don't like this, Klaus, not at all. Put your pants on and look for him down the road. Maria, you look in the stable and storeroom. I'll check with the Wilkins."

I heard Maria at the stable doorway, then heard her leave. After a few minutes I climbed down for another peek outside. It was too dark to see much, but I could hear Mother heading toward Mr. Wilkins' smokehouse — one of my hideouts when I was trying to escape a spanking. I decided to sneak over to Ned's house as soon as she was gone.

Suddenly there were footsteps right outside.

"Hans, where are you?" Maria called softly in her cutest tones. Then her voice rose to a coaxing whine. "Hans, where *are* you?"

I caught a glimpse of her silhouette as she passed the stable door. How I loved my little sister! I wanted to give her one last hug, one that would last me the entire war. I just couldn't leave without that.

"Maria," I called softly.

"Is that you, Hans?" she whispered.

"Shh! Yes, come here, Maria."

She approached slowly, then repeated, "Is that you, Hans?"

"Shh. Yes." I put my hand on her head.

She looked up to make sure it was I, then with the throat of a dozen witches screamed, "Mommy! Here's Hans!"

Well, that ended that!

The next day Ned told me he had gotten stuck doing the dishes, and with his huge family that took some time. But it became obvious he didn't really want to be a soldier. He even had the nerve to ask if the Baron would mind terribly if we became sailors instead!

As for Klaus, he couldn't touch me that night because Mother was too busy lecturing me on John Milton's quote:

"They also serve who only stand and wait." The next day, though, when she was over at the church rolling bandages for the wounded, Klaus cornered me in the bedroom. Since I had no room to display my dazzling skills in tactical maneuvers, I won't relate the dull details of that unfair battle.

14. Meeting of the Congregation

The July heat had been oppressive and unrelieved, yet the news from Virginia more than made up for it. On the 21st of the month our army had met the Yankees at the Manassas railroad junction, and in that first major battle of the war had utterly routed them.

According to the newspaper Union soldiers, baggage wagons, and even senators and ladies who had come to watch the battle went scampering all the way back to Washington, D. C. Everyone was in a delirium of happiness, feeling confident that the war was as good as won. The only cloud over our joy was the news that Mr. Mahlstedt had been seriously wounded.

Each passing day brought further glowing details of the battle. Ned and I spent our spare time trading the latest news of the victory. Besides the newspaper reports and the usual rumors, I had Reverend Mr. Koenig as a source of information.

He had been coming from Savannah to conduct services at our church once each month. Now, as a preacher he was nothing earthshaking. Mr. Dorow over at Jerusalem Church was much better. To be brutally honest, Mr. Koenig's sermons did more to put me to sleep than did the torrid afternoon heat. Yet while having supper at our house afterwards, he never failed to hold my attention. He always knew so much about the war — bits and scraps of information that had escaped the newspapers.

Then came my father's first letter since the battle. As usual Mother kept part of it for herself — "private stuff," she said. My page contained a lecture on running away and how Mother had grown up in Germany in a large, comfortable house with many servants and how life in America had been a great strain on her and she needed her brave warrior to help her or the burden would be too much for her. He wanted my promise that I would never again try to run away. An appropriate Bible quote was included. The only reference to the battle came in a postscript.

I saw Sam the other day in a hospital here. He had been badly wounded charging a Federal artillery position in the recent battle. I went back to see him this morning, but he was already dead. "I am the Resurrection and the Life," saith the Lord.

Why had I always spouted off about Sam's lack of courage? Now I wished I had told him that I was sorry. But I couldn't when I had the chance because I was too busy waiting for him to say that to me.

Well, we basked in the glory of Manassas all that summer and through most of the fall, but early in November, by which time lots of people thought Mr. Lincoln had called off his war, the Yankees forced a landing on Hilton Head Island, about 10 miles north of the Savannah's mouth. Soon afterwards they landed on Big Tybee Island at the very mouth of the river, only a dozen miles from Savannah itself. Their gunboats began blockading all the inlets, so that no ocean commerce could reach the city.

People in Savannah panicked. Many fled to cities deep in the interior. Others who couldn't afford to move that far sought refuge in the surrounding countryside, including Effingham County. So with the influx of refugees to our area, we experienced an immediate shortage of food and housing. Prices skyrocketed, and Mr. Hildebrandt chose this occasion to raise the price of our tuition.

The financial affairs of the congregation apparently were suffering too, because the first Sunday in December Mr. Dorow announced from the pulpit that the trustees wanted to meet with the entire congregation on the following Sunday. But what interested me was the other announcement—that the following Sunday Mr. Koenig would be preaching at our church.

I promised to tell Ned everything I could learn from him—about the deployment of the Yankees in the marshlands east of the city, about our forts along the river protecting the city, and about what our river fleet was doing to hold the Yankee navy at bay. I especially hoped to wangle Mr. Koenig into taking me with him to Savannah. There'd be so much to see—soldiers, troop trains, maybe even one of the river forts. With what impatience I awaited that Sunday!

It arrived at last in a cold drizzle. I had reluctantly helped Mother with the noon-meal dishes and was almost dressed for church when a soldier on horseback rode up to the house. He handed Mother a small package, then rode off again.

"Is it from Father?" I asked.

"No, a Major Greene."

"What's in it?"

She looked pale as she turned it over in her hands several times without opening it. "Private stuff," she said.

"A Christmas present, maybe?"

Mr. and Mrs. Hanser pulled up in their carriage, and Mother went out to see them.

"I thought I'd stop by to invite you all to the meeting after church," I heard Mrs. Hanser say.

"But the meetings aren't for women and children."

Mrs. Hanser's voice had that molasses acid about it.

"Well, this one concerns you all, dearie. I wouldn't want you to miss it for the world."

Mother came in quite upset and headed right for her bedroom. When she reemerged for church 20 minutes later, her eyes were all bloodshot.

"What are the Hansers up to?" I wondered. "They sure have Mother worked up."

Klaus pulled me out onto the porch.

"Now see what you've done! The fuss you made about helping with the dishes! Why don't you do what Father said?"

"It's not me!" I told him. "If anyone's to fault, it's the Hansers."

"Oh, sure, sure! Hans, you'll bring Mother to an early grave yet. Just mark my words!"

On the way to church she started to cry. Klaus reigned up the mare to see if Mother was all right, and I thought of apologizing for the fuss I had made about the dishes, but instead only asked, "Don't you feel well?"

She hid her face in her hands as her body quaked with sobs.

Now I felt sure it wasn't my behavior but something to do with the Hansers. I tried to change the subject.

"What was in the package?"

She began crying out loud.

"Oh, Hans," Klaus scolded, "why don't you just hush your mouth! You do nothing but upset her."

"No," Mother interrupted between sobs. "It's not your fault, Hans. Just go on." She had to break off to cry a bit more. Then she said, "When we get home, you can see the package. Maybe Pastor Koenig can explain it to you." She burst out crying once more, then composed herself as we drove up to the church.

The pews were more crowded than usual, a sign that people again felt a need to get God on our side, what with the Yankees being so close.

When I awoke from Reverend Koenig's sermon, he was announcing that Mr. Hanser and the trustees wanted the congregation to remain for the special meeting. Suddenly I felt we were on the verge of finding out what had upset Mother.

I never knew what all had transpired between the Hansers and my father. That they had no love for him I had sensed for a long time. Father and Mother never said a word about it in front of Klaus or me, but from time to time I overheard Miss Brennen, whom we called "Miss Julia," and other members talk about it. They would say, "Isn't it a shame what the Hansers are saying about Mr. Schmidt?" and things like that.

Many of the men were off with the army, but of those that remained not many stayed for the meeting. That didn't surprise me, since most of the congregation usually figured if the Hansers were sponsoring something, it would only lead to trouble. We of course stayed because of our special invitation.

Mr. Hanser was the speaker. "The trustees agreed to call this meeting because my wife and I — and several others who didn't want their names mentioned — have been discussing something that concerns you all. As you all know, Mr. Schmidt isn't serving us any more. Mr. Dorow and Mr. Koenig are. And I . . . I mean *we* — we all know the outrageous prices these days. You all pay them as well as me. So does the congregation. Well, we all'd better do something about it, or this here congregation is going to be in deep trouble."

The congregation applauded.

Mr. Hanser continued. "Well, we can't lower the prices none. So the problem is, how can we get more money to pay the prices?"

"What happened to the money we used to give Mr. Schmidt?" someone asked.

Mr. Hanser glared. "That's all eaten up, what with prices going sky-high and food so scarce. Inflation's eaten up all the interest on our church bonds too. But as I figure it, we got another source of income we ain't tapped yet. And it 'd be a tidy little sum too."

"Then let's tap it!" Mr. Speier called out. "But what is it?"

Mr. Hanser paused to size up the mood of the group. Everyone was waiting expectantly. "The parsonage," he announced.

Mother again buried her face in her hands.

Mr. Hanser continued in an overly loud voice, "That's salary, ain't it? For services we all ain't getting no more! It's a fine, substantial house, and we could rent it out for a tidy sum."

A fine substantial house! I recalled our first summer in that house — the bedbugs and my sleepless nights hunting through the bed sheets for those nocturnal crawlers, the broken shutters and steps, the broken-down chickenhouse and overgrown fence, and how we had fixed and remodeled the place into the substantial house it had now become, without a lick of help from the Hansers!

"But Pastor Schmidt is serving our country," Mr. Speier objected. "And the army can't pay him enough to provide housing for his family."

Pastor Koenig spoke up. "Don't treat your pastor and his family this way when he's off ministering to our soldiers."

Mr. Hanser was back on his feet. "Mr. Koenig, we all respect you as a servant of the Lord. But you didn't know Nathanael Bohlmann or Donald Mahlstedt."

"What about them?" Pastor Koenig asked.

"Casualties! And more are bound to come. More of our loyal sons giving their lives for their country."

"Mr. Hanser, I don't see . . . ."

He burst in again, "Why should we go on a-giving support to Mr. Schmidt? You all know how he felt about slavery. And have you all forgotten about Mr. Triebner, our pastor during the Revolution, and how he sold us out to the British? A traitor! Now we've got Mr. Schmidt! And I for one ain't fooled by the Confederate uniform! What's he underneath but a Yankee?"

A hushed murmur ran through the congregation. Then all was silent except for Mother's loud sobbing. I waited for someone to jump to his feet to defend Father.

"Well," Mr. Pieper reasoned slowly, "if they could stay on in the parsonage till after Christmas, till they can find another place, well, then it wouldn't be like we were taking the roof from over their heads."

More silence followed. Then Pastor Koenig said, "I think you all should hold off on this matter until Mr. Dorow and more of the members are present."

"What's to wait for?" Mr. Hanser said. "We can think for ourselves."

For a minute or more Mother couldn't get out any words. Klaus and I put our arms around her until she began to regain some control.

She rose to her feet and looked from face to face as she struggled for words. Again her whole body convulsed, and all she could finally manage was: "Keep your parsonage!" Then producing the opened package from her purse and flinging it on the floor, she grabbed Maria by the hand and fairly pulled her from the church, with Klaus tagging close behind.

Pastor Koenig called out, "Wait, Mrs. Schmidt! Wait!" But she kept on going.

I had some choice words to say to the group, so I stayed. Before I could find the voice to express what was boiling inside me, Mr. Speier picked up an army buckle that had fallen from the package. He then began to read aloud a letter that had been folded around it. In the letter a Major

Greene described how my father had ministered to the wounded on the battlefield at Manassas and how he had been twice cited for bravery, once for his courage on the battlefield and once for his ministry to soldiers taken with smallpox, typhus, and measles.

I was so swollen with pride I didn't notice that Mr. Speier had quit reading aloud. When I looked up, he was handing the letter to Mr. Hanser.

Mr. Hanser read it to himself, then went pale. I stood there for a few minutes taking great delight in watching each of them repent as the letter passed from one person to another. How wrong it proved them! My father, a traitor! Indeed! But the more faces I studied the less I enjoyed their suffering. Here and there I caught hard eyes growing misty, even teary. This ceased to be fun. Some readers looked downright stricken.

I started to grow anxious. When Mr. Pieper finished reading the letter, he groaned, "Father, forgive us. We didn't know what we were doing."

I ran over and grabbed the letter from his hand. I skipped over the part that had been read, then continued aloud:

> During this battle against ravaging diseases, which have done us far more mischief than any enemy bullets, your husband, while continuing to minister to the victims, I am most regretful to say, himself became a victim of measles and, on November 29 last, succumbed.

My knees buckled. "Father!" I cried.

"Lord, have mercy!" someone mumbled.

15. Fort Pulaski

I just knew it was nothing but a horrible dream from which I'd soon wake up. Yet it kept lingering, too long for a dream, and Mother's pain seemed too real. But it had to be a dream!

I could prove it. I walked outside in the rain. You don't feel rain in a dream. But the cold and the wet — I felt them, as real as the pain I thought I was dreaming. No dream.

Then maybe it was all a mix-up. Any hour another letter would arrive and declare the first a mistake. But as hours turned into days and no letter came, gradually I realized that Father wasn't coming back, and my pain grew. Four of us still lived in the house, yet it was empty. The four of us were in the same room, yet I was there all alone.

The following Saturday the congregation had a memorial service at Jerusalem Church. Mr. Koenig delivered the eulogy and Mr. Dorow a good sermon that helped me see things from Father's point of view. His death was a victory, because he wasn't really dead but alive and happy with the Lord, where bullets and disease and even barbed tongues could no longer hurt him.

After the service Mr. Hanser stood up and begged us to forgive him and the congregation and to stay on in the parsonage. When Mother hesitated, he pleaded that she reach no decision until after Christmas. To this she agreed.

I didn't see how Christmas that year could bring anything good, because the night before Maria found my marbles while hunting tree decorations in the storeroom. She asked me if they weren't mine, and I remembered. How I remembered our last Christmas together and cried!

When we returned from the Christmas service the following day we found Mr. Hanser — though not Mrs. — and many other parishioners waiting in front of the house. Mr. Hanser handed Mother the deed to the parsonage and to a 10-acre tract of land nearby. Then he led us to the kitchen storeroom where we found a barrel of flour, a large sack of rice, corn for a spring planting, and shelves piled high with home-canned goods. Out by the woodpile stood three cords of wood, and Mr. Hanser told us that our new field had a milk cow that now belonged to us, as did the mare and buggy.

What could Mother say? In a time of growing scarcity all this was more than a Christmas present. It represented the repentance of many people. It was their way of asking for forgiveness. And forgive them she did.

Two days earlier she had received a letter from the von Rohrs in Augusta, inviting us to come live with them. Mr. von Rohr was her cousin and had been responsible for our coming to America in the first place. She wanted to accept their invitation but told me afterwards, "The people here feel so guilty that just telling them all is forgiven isn't enough. We must *show* them. If we move away now, they'll feel more guilty than ever."

So we stayed.

Early the following spring Klaus and I plowed and planted our new field. Soon lush green corn shoots covered the ground, promising a good crop, but a sudden turn of events made Mother change her mind.

We got our first inkling of what was happening on the morning of April 10th. The day was cold and windy. Klaus and I had just set out for school when we heard what sounded like very distant thunder, except that instead of a rolling sound it was staccato. It continued throughout the day and at intervals through the night.

The following morning Mr. Hildebrandt told us that what we were hearing was Yankee artillery firing on Fort Pulaski, the brick structure I had seen when we first arrived in Georgia, guarding the mouth of the Savannah River. Later in the day the sound died away. Ned thought this was due to a shift in the wind, but over the weekend we were stunned to learn that the garrison in the fort had surrendered.

Mr. Hildebrandt treated us first thing Monday to a tirade against what he called the cravenly conduct of the garrison.

Then, great patriot that he was, he treated us to the announcement that henceforth he would accept tuition payments only in kind, no longer in Confederate currency.

For Mother this was the last straw. "The war is too close," she told Klaus and me. "I've already lost your father. I don't want to lose my children too. Besides, the congregation only gives us currency for your schooling. And with Maria at school age now, we could never afford paying Mr. Hildebrandt in kind. So we're moving to Augusta."

I was bitterly disappointed. Besides my friends, I would have to leave my chance to avenge myself on the Yankees, especially now that they were barely 30 miles away and Savannah was preparing for an all-out defense. Yet I couldn't argue with Mother, knowing as I did how much she was suffering because of Father's death.

By the following Thursday, the last school day before Easter, Mother had traded our buggy and cow for a farm wagon and an extra horse, and she was packing the wagon with as many of our possessions as it would hold. So I set off for school knowing that it would be my last day there.

As I looked around the schoolroom, my stomach churned, especially at the thought of leaving Ned and Sally Jo. Right then I decided to break my silence with Sally Jo, and I didn't care who laughed. Only I would have to wait for just the right moment.

"Hans!" Mr. Hildebrandt barked.

"Sir?"

"You weren't listening? Well, for *you* I'll repeat the question. If one Confederate soldier can kill nine Yankees, how many Confederates will it take to kill 81 Yankees?"

I made no reply.

"What's the matter, Hans? You don't know your division?"

"No, sir. I don't know the general."

This didn't set well with Mr. Hildebrandt.

A few minutes before 12 he put coffee on to brew so it would be ready by noon recess. This had come to be quite a ritual with him. Before the war he drank at least three cups a day—one during the morning recess, one at noon, and one during the afternoon recess. Sometimes also during class. Now with the Yankee blockade making coffee so scarce and with his refusal to use chickory as a substitute, he rationed himself to one cup a week, which he always drank on Fridays.

What a celebration he made of it! Usually he gave a speech on the joys of ending another week with the likes of us. So as he poured this week's cup, every eye was fastened on him.

"This week," he began, "my coffee will taste better than ever. I really have something to celebrate—the departure of Hans Schmidt."

He twisted his mouth a bit as he stirred the coffee. "Hans, I once said I'd make you or break you." He placed the spoon neatly beside the cup. "Well, I didn't make a man out of you, that's for sure. And now you're going to run off before I can break you. Well, I never did like you, not one bit! You know why?"

I was taken by utter surprise. I had misbehaved now and then like the other boys, but I had no idea he had a dislike for me over and beyond his dislike for most people in general.

"No, sir," I answered.

"Because you always got good grades without studying hard. And now because you're running away from the Yankees. But most of all, because you're your father's son, and I never liked him or his attitude at all. In any case, I'll be glad to see your back. That goes for you too, Klaus."

I sat there immobilized as he gave the coffee one final, ceremonial stir, neatly laid the spoon back down beside the cup, and announced: "Class dismissed!"

His saying that I was running from the Yankees stabbed deep, but what he said about Father nearly ripped the heart out of me. Through my tears I saw Mr. Hildebrandt's malevolent sideburns join his mustache in one mighty, mocking sneer. Suddenly it dissolved and I saw Father standing before me on the train platform. His eyes were dancing and he reached out a hand to shake mine. I extended my hand, but that bushy sneer returned, blotting Father out, except for his buckle. I saw just the buckle, then the letter, and then that mocking sneer again. "I never liked him at all, at all, at all."

A rage swept through me as I wiped my eyes on my sleeves. I got up to leave but noticed the cup of coffee still steaming on Mr. Hildebrandt's desk. My eyes fell upon the box of salt on the shelf behind his desk, then they roved around the classroom. It was empty. My hands nimbly scooped four heaping teaspoons of the salt into the cup and gave it a stir.

As I hurried out into the damp spring air, I brushed against Mr. Hildebrandt coming through the doorway. He growled. Outside I saw Sally Jo looking at me expectantly. Suddenly it came to me that I had the courage to speak to her. I stepped forward and said, "Sally Jo?"

Her eyes turned deep as an autumn sky and her lips formed to speak.

"Yaah! Phoo! Phoo!" I heard from inside. Then came the explosion. "Who did it? Who did it?"

Sally Jo looked apprehensive, as if she knew who was about to be the victim of Mr. Hildebrandt's wrath. "Sally Jo," I repeated just as the wave of sound hit me with gale force.

"Hans Schmidt!" It echoed like a deep-throated thunder from inside the schoolhouse.

With that my legs started to churn, and before I knew it, I was on my way home. Looking back, though, I could see him on the school steps shaking his fist. Even beyond the bend in the road I could hear him bellowing, "Hans Schmidt! You come back! Hear? You come back!"

Mother met me at the kitchen door. "Hans, what are you doing home so early?"

"I . . . I wanted . . . to help you," I told her breathlessly.

"There's always time for school."

Her eyes smiled. "I declare, Hans, you can be so considerate when you want to." Then she frowned. "But maybe Mr. Hildebrandt wanted to say good-bye. He'll be hurt."

"Not half as much as I'd be," was my reply.

"I hate good-byes too," she nodded, thinking that she understood my meaning. "Come and help me pack."

On Good Friday and Easter I looked for Sally Jo at services, but apparently her parents took her to Jerusalem Church over by the river landing.

Several members showed up Monday morning to see us off. They told Mother they would hold the property in trust for us in case we should return one day.

Ned showed up too. He had to skip school to do it, but then as he put it: "No sacrifice is too much for a pal. Besides, I reckon I can forget about school. I'm 14 now, and my folks has said I can join up if I wants to. And I powerful wants to."

"The navy?"

"I'm leaning toward the idea. I suppose I can't get a seagoing ship what with the blockade and all, but I can get me a fighting river boat and that's good enough."

Then he lifted Tag up onto my lap. "I wants for you to keep him, Hans."

"No, Ned. I can't do that. He's your dog."

"Shucks, ain't no allowing a old hound dog in the navy. And I can't just leave him behind. I knows you'll take good care of him, and maybe he'll whine lots when you drive off, but he'll get over me and be you one fine hound dog. Ain't that so, Tag?"

Tag barked his agreement, and Ned's eyes welled with tears.

Klaus urged the horses forward and we were on our way, to what I didn't know. When I looked back, the house had disappeared beyond the bend, and something of my life with it.

Back in the distance Ned reappeared, running and waving. Tag looked back and whined.

"He'll be you a good hound dog, Hans!" Ned was crying but somehow managed to get out, "You all . . . come back . . . some day! Hear? He shouted it once more extra loud. "Hear?"

16. The Warehouse Fire

The spring rains had transformed the road at many points into a quagmire. Fortunately, we had joined a small wagon train of refugees in Springfield; so when any wagon became mired, we all pitched in to pull it free. But as we neared Augusta, this became increasingly difficult because the sandy roads turned to a red clay that sucked at and gobbled up horses' hoofs and wagon wheels alike. In a number of spots we had to fell timber to corduroy the road before we could go on.

When our creaking, mud-caked wagons finally lumbered into Augusta, we found the city in a state of jitters. Soldiers were on guard everywhere — at the arsenal and warehouses, around the powder works and cotton mills, by the railroad depot and the bridge across the Savannah. We discovered that several weeks earlier Yankee spies had stolen a train and used it to wreck track and bridges of the Western and Atlantic Railroad north of Atlanta. The spies had been captured, but now rumors about more Yankee spies set the whole state on edge. Teamsters driving wagonloads of cotton and tobacco into Augusta added to the alarm by reporting that bushwhackers were taking shots at them.

All this merely stimulated my excitement and, in spite of missing Ned and Sally Jo, I liked Augusta right away. For one thing, the von Rohr house was like a palace compared to our parsonage. The outside was painted, and the inside walls had plaster and wallpaper and even gas lamps. The parlor swallowed up a piano, sofa, writing desk, and numerous glassed-in bookcases with room to spare. Best of all, the house had five bedrooms, and since the von Rohrs' older son was in the army and both daughters were married, one to a Yankee merchant and the other to a Charleston mechanic, three bedrooms were vacant. So I no longer had to share a bedroom with Klaus.

The von Rohrs were nice too, especially Mr. von Rohr. Shortly after we arrived, he saw me looking at the set of 10 tin soldiers on his writing desk, and right away he sensed what I felt about them. So without batting an eyelash he gave them to me. I didn't play with them, having outgrown that sort of thing, but placed them on my dresser where I could admire them and dream.

What I liked best about Augusta was the fact that the war had forced prices so high there that Mother couldn't afford to send us to school. To earn some money, she privately tutored some students, but this didn't bring in enough money. So the only lessons we had to suffer through were those she gave us at home.

Augusta did have one serious drawback. Carl von Rohr was only 8 years old—too young to be my companion—so I had to adjust to the idea of having my older brother for a friend.

By summer I had found another friend—of sorts, at least. His name was John Kraft, a skinny giant who was self-willed and overbearing, always wanting and getting his own way. Yet Mother liked him because he was well-groomed and always polite and proper in the presence of adults, saying "Yes, sir" and "No, ma'am." Just what mothers seem to want most in their sons' friends!

John took soldiering as seriously as I did, maybe even more so. He taught me to make a big map for my bedroom wall and to mark on it the dispositions of all armies in the field, at least insofar as we could glean this information from the daily newspapers.

As 1862 gave way to 1863 though, life in Augusta began to lose its charm. The spy fever had died down, and prices were soaring out of sight, causing Mother to lose all her students. She went to work in the textile mill, but even her new income was not enough in this time of runaway inflation. So Klaus and I had to look for work too.

Mr. von Rohr found jobs for us at the Confederate States Powder Works, where he worked as a chemist. This network of brick buildings, which sprawled for two miles on both sides of the Augusta canal, manufactured much of the gunpowder used by our armies. At first Klaus and I embraced our work with enthusiasm because it was helping our war effort, but we soon found it taxing and dull, and longed for the days at the old schoolhouse.

What was worse, our pay couldn't keep up with the prices. I earned 12 dollars a week, but this wouldn't buy even one gallon of molasses and was barely enough for half a bushel of sweet potatoes. One cord of firewood cost me almost four weeks' wages.

By early summer, though, we thought our hardships were almost over. General Lee had soundly thrashed the Yankees at Chancellorsville, Virginia, and had followed this by invading Pennsylvania. We expected that our armies would soon be returning victorious, but in July Lee's invasion of the North recoiled in defeat from a town called Gettysburg. Right on top of that we learned that the gallant defenders of Vicksburg, our last fortress on the Mississippi, had surrendered.

Up to this time people had borne the hardships without complaint, but now they began to grumble about our generals, the shortages, the prices. And when five Yankee officers escaped from a prisoner-of-war camp in Macon, Georgia, Augusta went wild with rumors. The escapees were seen headed toward Augusta. They were hiding *in* Augusta. They were plotting to blow up the arsenal and the powder works.

One night a cotton warehouse by the river burned to the ground. "The escapees did it!" the newspaper reported, and proved it by pointing to the chemical origin of the fire. The next day, though, the five escapees were captured near Valdosta, about 200 miles to the south.

The newspaper now blamed the fire on Union spies. It said someone had overheard the spies on the night of the fire talking in German outside the warehouse.

Secret service agents came by and questioned Mother and the von Rohrs. When they learned that Father had died serving in the Confederate army, they quit questioning Mother but took Mr. von Rohr to the jail for further questioning.

How could they suspect a man like him? He spoke German, but so what? Lots of people did. And he was a chemist. What did that prove? And did his having a Yankee son-in-law make him a Union sympathizer? He also had a son risking his life with Lee.

The secret police apparently saw things as I did and after two days released him. But obviously somewhere in the city a spy was on the loose, because the night after Mr. von Rohr's release a second cotton warehouse went up in flames. And again the fire was of chemical origin.

17. Hidden Revolver

Mr. von Rohr was a descendant of the Baron too, so from time to time we talked about our illustrious ancestor. He told me a few anecdotes about him but knew nothing about his military exploits. Still, talking about the Baron re-kindled my ambition to be a soldier.

I was 15 and a half years old now, an age at which many boys became drummers in the army, but Mother's health kept me from asking her for permission. Besides her arduous hours at the textile mill, she and Mrs. von Rohr worked at home till late in the night manufacturing many necessities no longer available in the stores. They got down an ancient spinning wheel from the attic, and Mother rediscovered the practically lost arts of home carding, spinning, and weaving. She also drained lye from ashes and mixed it with refuse grease to make soap. She pulverized charcoal for tooth powder and converted old pillow cases and drapes into blouses and dresses. Then too she had endless meetings at the church—to knit socks for the soldiers or to serve at socials for soldiers on leave or to visit children orphaned by the war.

The long hours and meager diet had told so noticeably on her health that, besides giving up temporarily the idea of joining the army, I looked for ways to help her, and I quit asking her to do for me things I could do myself.

Klaus and I had started taking instructions for confirmation, but because of the paper shortage we could not get a catechism. Mr. von Rohr said his older son Frederick's catechism was somewhere about and that we were welcome to use it. We found it in one of the bookcases, but its covers were missing and the binding had come unstitched.

Mother offered to hunt up some old board and paper to make new covers with.

"You have more than enough to do," I told her. "Go on with your knitting and I'll do the looking."

I knew there was none in the house, but as yet I had not been down in the cellar. I lit a candle to explore it.

"Couldn't you wait for morning?" Mother called. "That's almost the last candle we have."

"I won't be long. Klaus can search with me, so we'll not use up much of it."

Klaus grumbled but went with me. Along the near wall of the cellar sat a crock of collard-green sauerkraut — the last Mrs. von Rohr would make for some time, the cost of salt being what it was. Next to it were a bushel of sweet potatoes and an empty flour barrel. Along the opposite wall stood several shelves lined with fruit jars. Most of these were empty, except on the top shelf. There we found canned peaches and molasses and what looked like liquor bottles.

"Hey," I told Klaus, "isn't that brandy up there?"

"So what if it is?"

"You ever had some?"

"No, and you're not going to either."

"Didn't say I was! Just help me turn this barrel over. Maybe we can take a sniff at least."

"No. What if Mr. von Rohr comes?"

"Oh, it'll just take a second or two! He'll never know."

I turned the barrel over by myself.

"This ain't finding what we were looking for, Hans."

"Well, there's no cloth or paper down here, that's sure. And there's no sense letting the candle go to complete waste."

I stood on top of the barrel and pulled down a bottle for closer inspection.

"Hurry up. I think I hear Mr. von Rohr coming."

I hurried to put the bottle back when I noticed something lying behind the bottles.

"There's something here. Hold this bottle for me."

"What is it? Can't you hurry up?"

I pulled it out and held it up.

"Hey, what's a revolver doing here?" Klaus asked in a hushed voice.

"I don't know. It's a Colt 44." I turned it over. "And, Klaus," I whispered, "look at this!"

He read the inscription on the barrel: "U. S. ARMY. What's a Yankee gun . . .?" He stopped. "Hssst. Someone's coming."

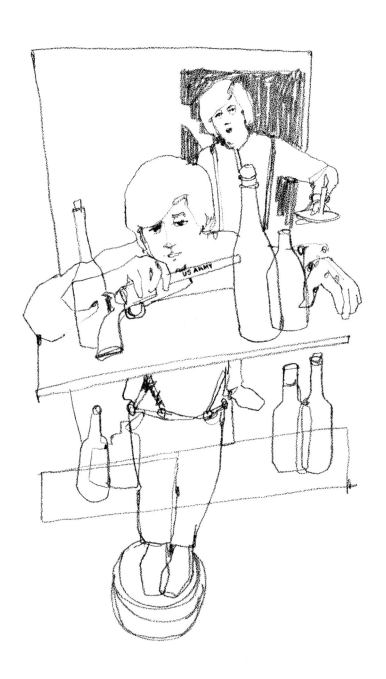

I hurriedly put the revolver back. Klaus was handing me the bottle when the cellar door opened.

"Hans, are you down there?" The voice belonged to Mr. von Rohr. "You better come up. There's nothing down there but some food and empty jars. I've already looked. Hans?"

"Yes, sir?"

"You're just wasting the candle."

"Yes, sir. I'm coming." I slid the bottle back in its place and climbed down from the barrel.

He started down the steps, but Klaus and I hurried to intercept him.

"Don't be wasting a candle on the cellar. Nothing here to look for. Right?"

"Yes, sir. I mean, no sir."

Saturday as Klaus and I walked over to the church for confirmation instructions we swore John Kraft to secrecy, then told him about the revolver.

"Maybe Mr. von Rohr's the Yankee Spy," John said.

"He can't be," I answered. "He wouldn't help the people who killed my father."

"Measles killed Father," Klaus corrected.

"Maybe he got the gun from the arsenal," I suggested. "It used to be a Federal arsenal, didn't it?"

"Now, why would they give *him* a revolver?" Klaus said scornfully.

"Well, maybe his son Frederick captured it off a dead Yankee and sent it home as a trophy."

"You don't hide trophies," John observed. Then he made us recount how Mr. von Rohr acted when he found us in the cellar.

That's when the horrible thought struck me. "We forgot to turn the barrel back over!"

"Oh! Oh! What if he goes down there and sees it?" Klaus asked.

"Another thing," John said. "What time did you say he came home last night?"

"About 10."

"Where was he?"

"At work. He works late a lot."

"I'll bet! Did you see today's paper?"

"No. What?"

"Another warehouse fire last night, that's what. And it broke out about nine. He's your spy, all right. You better report him."

"No!" I insisted. "He can't be. He's too nice."

"Besides," said Klaus, "if we report him, it'd kill Mother. John, you promised to keep this a secret."

"I will, don't you fret none about that, but I'm telling you where your duty lies."

When we reached the church, I invited John to come in.

"No. Ain't allowed."

"Because you're Catholic?"

"Ain't that. My father says we ain't having no more truck with church."

"Why not?"

"Because God doesn't answer our prayers."

"How do you know He doesn't?"

"Look at the way the war's going, and all. If He is, my father and I don't like His answers none."

I began to wonder if John's attitude was general and maybe explained why our church attendance had fallen off so badly. Our pastor always prayed for victory and for the conversion of the godless Yankees and even made God out to be the personal Champion of the Confederacy. If God was, it did seem He was bungling the job pretty badly and didn't deserve to be worshiped anymore. But somehow I couldn't imagine God choosing up sides in our war.

During the weeks that followed John kept bringing up the matter of the revolver, and I kept insisting Mr. von Rohr couldn't be a spy. His son Frederick had sent him the gun and, however peculiarly placed, the gun was a trophy, nothing more.

Not long after, Frederick came home on leave. So I had a chance to prove my belief. I plied him with questions about the war, general questions that I wasn't afraid to ask in front of his father. But one morning when we were alone, I grew bold.

"I'll bet you've collected lots of souvenirs off dead Yankees."

"No, not really. Sometimes I've taken something I've needed."

"Like what?"

"Oh, some coffee or matches or a pair of boots!"

"And a revolver?"

"Yes, lots of us have taken revolvers."

"And sent it home as a trophy?"

"A trophy?" He laughed. "Heavens, no! Maybe when the war's over. Right now a body's got use for such a trophy at the front."

At that moment my love for Mr. von Rohr turned into suspicion. Shortly after Frederick had returned to the front, I sneaked into the cellar to right the barrel but someone — and not Klaus — had beat me to it, and my suspicion changed to fear.

On Palm Sunday, 1864, Klaus and I were confirmed. The pastor preached on the text: "Thou therefore endure hardness as a good soldier of Jesus Christ." He made it plain that "soldier of Jesus" meant "soldier of the Confederacy" and spoke with considerable warmth about doing our duty toward our country. Though what Father had taught me made me doubt such an interpretation of the text, still the sermon did disturb my conscience. What Klaus had said though — that our reporting Mr. von Rohr would kill Mother — disturbed me still more.

That evening Mother asked me why I so seldom talked to Mr. von Rohr. "It seems obvious to me that you are deliberately avoiding him," she said, "and I want to know why."

What could I tell her?

"It's rude, Hans. It's bad manners and terribly ungrateful after all he's done for us. And, believe me, I'm not alone in noticing your behavior. He's noticed it too."

My heart almost quit as I stammered, "How do you know?"

"Because he has questioned me at some length about it."

My feelings toward him turned to absolute terror.

18. A Powerful Thirst for Chocolate

One day Mr. von Rohr caught me on the stairs coming down from my bedroom. I nearly panicked.

"Hans," he said, "your mother seems overly tired and unhappy. Let's see if we can't do something to lift her spirits. I know a store where you can get some coffee."

"Coffee, sir?"

"Coffee. It'll cost us dearly, but maybe it'll do your mother some good."

He gave me 15 dollars and directions; so taking Tag with me, I set off for the store.

I stopped along the way to get John, who said he had heard of the store and its proprietor, Mr. Wind. "It's a small store, just recently opened up," he told me. "But it's always crowded with customers because Mr. Wind always has things nobody can get anywhere else. Salt and coffee and tea and sugar. How he comes by such things with the Yankee blockade and all nobody knows. Folks hate him because of the prices he charges."

I disliked Mr. Wind immediately when I noticed he had the same beady eyes and black mustache that Mr. Hildebrandt did. While I stood in line to be waited on, John looked about the shop.

"Hey, Hans," he pointed. "Look!"

I followed his finger and spotted something I hadn't seen in years — a box of chocolate. My parents used to treat us to a cup of steaming chocolate on Christmas. It was too expensive to have more often than that, but since the war even that once-a-year treat had come to an end. John and I stood there recalling every cup of chocolate we had ever drunk, and as our recollections piled up, our thirst for chocolate grew.

Our wait in line went for nothing because Mr. Wind wanted 20 dollars for a pound of coffee and wouldn't sell me less than a pound.

"I told you about him, didn't I?" John whispered to me. Then he said aloud, "How much for that there box of chocolate?"

"Boy, that's the only chocolate this side of Lee's Virginians," Mr. Wind answered, barely peeking over his spectacles. "Imported from France. Right under the guns of the whole darn Yankee navy. Forty dollars."

"Forty dollars! For that small box? It'd only make six cups!"

"That's more than most folks have tasted in years, and a half pound of sugar comes with it. You all don't have to buy it if you don't like the price. Somebody else will."

"I'll give you my belt," John offered as he unbuckled it and laid it on the counter. "And my knife too."

"No deal."

"No deal? You can sole a pair of shoes with the belt. Worth forty dollars easy."

I quickly added what I could: "Here's my suspenders."

Mr. Wind rocked with laughter. "You boys sure have a powerful thirst for chocolate! Sorry, boys. I don't trade except in currency."

"But everybody trades goods nowadays," John protested. "Worth more than all that paper money."

"Not everybody. Not me. Currency only. Forty dollars to be exact."

John angrily pulled his hat down over his head and turned for the door muttering, "He's just what folks say!" He stopped by the potbelly stove which, because the weather was unseasonably cold for April, was lit and cooking merrily. He started to put on his belt but suddenly looked back at Mr. Wind, who was busy with another customer. Quick as a wink John opened the stove door and fed the fire with his belt. Leaving the door open a crack, he stood there until we could smell the aroma of the burning leather. "Just fine," he sniffed, and hurried outside, breaking into laughter. Then abruptly he turned serious. "I'm not done with Mr. Wind yet!"

"What you going to do?" I asked. "You've already wasted a valuable belt."

"Don't know yet." He stood there studying the store. "I've got it!" he said at last. "Will you help me?"

"Do what?"

He didn't have time to answer. We heard a commotion in the store, a sure clue that Mr. Wind wasn't as pleased as John with the aroma of burning leather. We tore down the street as fast as we could.

Back at his house John explained his further plans for Mr. Wind. I went for the idea, so that night we set out for the store with a small pail of paint and a brush. The lights in the store were out and the street deserted except for two soldiers. We waited until they disappeared from sight. Then Tag and I stood lookout while John went to work. His penmanship was rushed and sloppy, but when he was done, the sign on the window which had read "R. S. Wind Store" now read "R. S. Swindler's Store." He took a few moments to admire his handiwork, then we took off, figuring that was the end of our episode with Mr. Wind and the chocolate, but it wasn't.

Saturday John, Tag, and I went possum hunting in a field beyond town. The field had probably been a farm once but was now completely overgrown with tangled second growth. It wasn't the best place to hunt possum, but John didn't care what he shot. He was simply practicing his shooting and pretending he was stalking Yankees, while I was outwitting the Yankees with spectacular maneuvers. Up ahead we saw a large patch thick with scrubby pines. We stole into it to outflank our enemies. Deeper and deeper we plowed until we stumbled onto a board and batten shack that had pines growing practically up to its doorway and that had all its windows boarded up. Obviously the place had been deserted for some time.

I cautiously lifted the doorlatch, as if inside we'd catch the Yankee headquarters staff. John covered me with his rifle. I thrust the door open and rushed inside. Empty! But from the little light that came through the doorway we could see that the room was empty except for a table over in the darkest corner. It had some sort of contraption on it.

"Looks like a printing press," I suggested.

John went over to inspect it. "Look!" he said in an excited but hushed tone. He produced a stack of paper that in the dim light looked like dollars. We hurried to the door.

"It *is* money!" he exclaimed.

I read the inscription to make sure. "Richmond, April 6th, 1863. The Confederates States of America will pay Fifty Cents to the bearer."

John counted the stack in his hand. "There's a 100 of them. That's 50 dollars. And there's lots more in there too — nice, crispy, new currency. Hey!" he frowned. "That press! They all must be counterfeit! Oh, but who'll know the difference! Let's get some more."

"But it's against the law. It could hurt our country and make us lose the war. Don't you think . . . ."

"No time to think, except about the chocolate."

Tag's ears went up and he let out a low growl. I motioned to John. "Shh! He hears something."

John and I strained our ears. Then we heard it. Twigs snapping. Someone was coming.

I sneaked the door shut. Then we slipped back through the pines until we could no longer see the shack. We stopped to listen. The footsteps were quite close now. I cocked the hammer on my rifle. Suddenly the crunch of pine needles changed to a heavy tread on floorboards. "He's gone inside," I whispered. "Let's get out of here." We stole away ever so quietly until we were some distance from the shack. Then we victors over countless Yankees fled like a race horse with its tail on fire.

At John's house we resumed our debate over the money. "We should report it," I said. "You always told me it was my duty to report Mr. von Rohr."

"Well, that's different."

"Why?"

"'Cause it is. Besides, you didn't report him. So why should I report this! Fifty dollars, Hans," he added with great emphasis. "Fifty dollars! More than enough for the chocolate."

"But counterfeit dollars. That's cheating!"

"Ain't cheating to cheat a cheat. Besides, think of the chocolate!"

That powerful thirst came over me again and my patriotism weakened. "Well, I guess we could always report the counterfeiting press tomorrow — after we've bought the chocolate." My conscience remained unsatisfied until I added: "But we've got to share the chocolate with my mother!"

John readily agreed to this; so late that afternoon we entered the Wind store, though the sign still read "Swindler's Store."

Only one man was in line ahead of us. "Let's see," Mr. Wind calculated, "two pounds of coffee, a half pound of tea, one pound of sugar. That'll be $80 even."

"Hmmm. Maybe I'm forgetting something," the customer said as he looked around the store. "Oh, yes! How much for that box of chocolate?"

"From France, with a half pound of sugar to go with it. I'll make you a special bargain. Forty dollars."

"I'll take it!"

"You can't do that!" John protested. "I was going to buy it."

"Sorry. I already has." The man laid two $100 bills on the counter.

"That's 100," said Mr. Wind. "You owe me 20 more."

"No, no. See, there's 200 here," the customer corrected him.

Mr. Wind held up one of the bills. "It says 'State of Mississippi.' On their notes I give you 50 cents to the dollar, no more."

"Why, that's robbery!"

"Then go buy elsewhere."

"All right. Fifty dollars for the Mississippi note. But look at the other one. It's a Georgia note."

"Fifty cents to the dollar," Mr. Wind repeated.

"On a Georgia note?" the customer protested. "Don't you give a dollar on a dollar ever?"

"Yep, on Richmond currency, but only on Richmond."

"I'll buy the chocolate, then!" John interrupted.

Mr. Wind looked at him and chuckled. "You again? With what? Your belt? Or maybe it's disappeared, gone up in smoke, so to speak!"

"I don't know what you're talking about!" John said, making sure that his coat was buttoned so his beltless waist wasn't exposed. "But I've got money this time. Forty dollars. *Richmond* dollars."

"I can get more money," the customer objected, "and I was here first."

"I'll pay 50 dollars!" John volunteered.

"Well now, that's the kind of trading I like," said Mr. Wind.

"Wait!" the customer pleaded. "I'll give you 60. I don't have it with me, but I can get it by tonight."

"By tonight I'll get you 70," said John.

Mr. Wind rubbed his chin. "That's a lot of money."

"I'll make it 80!" said the customer, raising his voice.

"Eighty dollars?" Mr. Wind asked. "All right, 80 it is! Yes, that's a fair price. Eighty dollars Richmond. And to show you how fair I am I'll sell the chocolate to the first one who brings me 80, ah, no, 90 dollars Richmond."

"Fair enough!" John shouted and ran out the door.

I caught him and asked, "Where are you going to get the rest of the money?"

"The same place I got these. C'mon."

I tried to argue, but he brought up those memories of hot chocolate, and my thirst came back. "All right, but first I've got to tell my mother I'll be late for supper."

John figured this might delay us too long, so he went back inside and whispered to Mr. Wind that the other customer might get back first, but if Mr. Wind would hold off selling the chocolate, John would pay 150 dollars for it when he got back.

It was nearly dark by the time we reached the field of sapling pines. "What if the counterfeiter's there?" I asked.

"We'll see," John answered. "Let's move quietly."

We slipped among the pines with even greater stealth than when we were "soldiering." When the shack came into view, Tag stopped and aimed his nose and tail as if pointing out a possum.

"He must be in there," I said.

"Just our luck!"

We could hear the counterfeiter walking around inside. Then he emerged from the doorway and plowed through the pines not a dozen feet from us. John motioned to me, but I didn't understand what he was trying to tell me.

When the counterfeiter was gone, he said with almost a rage in his voice, "Did you see him?"

"His trousers, that's all. Did you?"

"Yes. Know who it was? The man in the store! The one trying to buy the chocolate. The crook! No wonder he could afford 90 dollars Richmond!"

We searched the shack but found all the money gone.

"Well, we'll never be able to pay more than he can now," I said. feeling more relieved than disappointed.

Suddenly John started laughing. "You know," he said between laughs, "that crook . . . is going to cheat . . . the swindler!"

Instead of going directly home we meandered over to the store. Neither of us said that that's where we were going. I suppose our thirst led us there. We peered in the window and to our surprise saw no counterfeiter; in fact, no customers at all—just Mr. Wind painting a sign.

Then I spied the box of chocolate and cried, "It's still there! See? On the shelf!"

"How come?" John wondered.

Curiosity led us inside.

"Ah, back with 150 dollars, boys?" Mr. Wind asked.

"Nope. Couldn't get the money," John answered.

"Didn't that man come back with his money?"

"Yes, he came back all right."

"Well, the box of chocolate—did you have another box?"

"No, it's the same box." Mr. Wind resumed his painting.

"The man changed his mind?" John pried.

"Of sorts. He decided to take a trip." Mr. Wind peered over the top of his spectacles. "To prison. See, he tried to pay me with counterfeit money." He straightened up, laid down his brush, then added, "Government agents arrested him, oh, scarce 10 minutes ago!"

My knees trembled, and I could see John's hands shake. He stuffed them into his coat pockets. Mr. Wind walked over to the shelf, fetched the box of chocolate, and held it out to us. "How about 40 dollars?" he asked.

"No!" John and I both answered.

"Thirty?"

We shook our heads.

"Twenty? Ten? Five? Not even five?" he asked with an air of surprise.

We shook our heads furiously.

"Well, tell you what. It's yours. Free."

"Free?"

"Yes, call it a going-out-of-business gift."

I took the box since John's hands seemed too badly burned by the counterfeit bills he was squeezing in his pocket.

"How come you're going out of business?" I asked.

"My work's done." He held up the sign he had been painting. It said "Closed."

"Your work?"

"Where do you think I was getting all these goodies from?"

We shrugged our shoulders.

"From the government in Richmond. I've been working for them, charging real high prices, hoping that one day the counterfeiter would show up to buy something. Well, this evening he did. In the nick of time too. A few more days and I would've had to give up. The way prices been rising, he couldn't have printed the stuff fast enough to pay for my wages here."

"What about this afternoon?" I asked. "Those notes he gave you . . . ."

"That was real money, but not tonight." Mr. Wind stepped out from behind the counter. "I sure hope no one else tries to pass counterfeit money around here."

John cleared his throat and shuffled his feet. I thanked Mr. Wind for the chocolates and we hurried to leave.

"Oh, by the way, boys," he called after us, "I sure wish I could find out who put that smelly belt in the stove and touched up the sign! I wanted to thank them. That's the way citizens should treat a storekeeper who uses war as an excuse to — ah — swindle people."

That night we built a fire kindled with 100 counterfeit notes and over it cooked hot chocolate for Mother and the family. In joyful spirit Mother offered thanks for Mr. Wind's unexpected generosity, but John and I were still too scared to drink any of the chocolate, especially since Mr. von Rohr sat down for a cup too.

19. Across the Chattahoochee

The summer of 1864 burned like a furnace, making my days at the powder works almost unbearable. At night I still had Mr. von Rohr to worry about, though my fear of him was now mixed with pity because he walked about with an infinite sadness in his eyes. Back in May he had received word that his son Frederick had been killed at Spottsylvania.

I began to wish we were back in Effingham County. At least we would have been able to grow enough food there to maintain ourselves. The irony of it all was that since our leaving there 27 months earlier the Yankees had become so bogged down in the salt marshes east of Savannah that they had not advanced more than a mile or two toward the city.

Elsewhere it was different. When I began my bedroom battle map, the blue scraps I used to represent Yankee armies stretched along much of the Mississippi. Now they formed a solid row along its entire length, and a second line of blue scraps had snaked its way along the Tennessee River, through Chattanooga, and on through the mountains of north Georgia until it stretched all the way to the Chattahoochee River near Atlanta.

We were assured that our defenses along the river would hold, but in no time at all the Yankees were across and our army was retreating into the entrenchments around Atlanta. Things would be different from now on, we were assured, because Hood, a real fighting general, had replaced General Johnston as commander of our army.

Through July and August the two armies sparred around the city, and it did seem that General Sherman's Yankee hordes had finally been fought to a standstill, as had Grant's hordes in Virginia. The newspapers said the North was weary of the war and in November would elect a president willing to make peace with us. But I had lost faith in what the newspapers said. All too often they would report a great victory by one of our armies, but a few days later their maps would show our victorious army further south, not north.

Mother told me that if Atlanta fell she would consider returning to Effingham County. I was in favor of the idea, because we would get away from Mr. von Rohr and from the scarcity. But I wondered about Sally Jo. How much had she changed? Would she still like me? She seemed to even after that book episode. So I guessed she would still. Then something happened to make me have doubts.

On a sultry Sunday afternoon late in August Klaus and I went over to John's house. He was in his yard, lounging against a pine, talking to two girls.

"Hey, John!" I called. "We're going for a walk over to the river. Want to come along?"

"Can't. Got company — my cousins. Well, not real cousins. We just call each other that. C'mon and meet them."

I saw long blonde hair and a cute turned-up nose. My heart nearly sprang into my mouth. "Sally Jo!" I said to myself. "It's Sally Jo!"

"Hans, Klaus, meet Susan Ann and Alice Beth."

"Hi," they said, stepping toward us.

"Hi," I answered, swallowing my disappointment.

"They're from Atlanta," John added. "They say the city's full of wounded soldiers. But we're whupping the Yankees good and proper."

I was about to ask them about the fighting around Atlanta when Susan Ann said, "You go along, John. We don't want to keep you all from your walk."

"No, I can't do that," he replied in a most chivalrous manner.

Another look at Susan Ann and I knew why he couldn't do that. She sure was pretty! So much like Sally Jo must look now.

"Of course you can," she insisted. "I'd feel downright guilty if you all stayed on our account."

John thought for a moment. "Well, I'll go if you all come along."

They both agreed, and the five of us set out together. They were such good company that it was silly to go crashing through all the heavy growth to reach the river. So instead we stopped by the banks of Lake Olmsted, a little sliver of a lake whose waters had taken on the red hue of the surrounding clay. We sat there dangling our bare feet in the water, chatting. Susan Ann was telling me about the war when John interrupted. "You know, I never kissed a girl before. Have you girls ever kissed a boy?"

Susan Ann and Alice Beth blushed and giggled. "No, silly," Alice Beth answered shyly.

John wasn't shy. "Well, I bet it'd be fun. What say we try it? Us boys can kiss you girls and then you all can vote on who kisses best."

He waited for an answer, but the girls just tugged at their skirts, made hoopless by the war, and giggled. So he volunteered, "I'll be first." He rose to his feet, drew each of the girls to a standing position and, bold as you please, kissed each of them in turn. I could hardly believe it; they didn't protest — just giggled a bit, both before and after, but were quite cooperative. So I got in line. Well, what would they think if I didn't? Besides, Susan Ann looked so much like Sally Jo!

After Klaus came my turn. I approached Susan Ann first. That's the first I noticed the problem. I stood on my tiptoes but was still having difficulties. Just as I was about to kiss her, she laughed and said, "Oh, Hans, you're so little!"

"Well, I don't have my shoes on," I said lamely. What a stupid thing to say! She didn't have hers on either.

"Why don't you stand on that there log," she invited sweetly.

I stood on it and kissed her but was so embarrassed I didn't enjoy the kiss at all, and right off I discovered that she wasn't so pretty. In fact she was kind of homely, nothing like Sally Jo. How come I hadn't noticed that before?

John wanted the girls to vote, but they just kept giggling. I didn't care whether they voted or not. "I'll never kiss a girl again," I told myself, "not as long as I live."

All the way home Susan Ann kept chattering away at me as if she didn't know how she had hurt me. And she acted as if she no longer noticed how short I was. Had she forgotten? Was she as stupid as she was ugly?

That night I told Mother what had happened. She laid down her carding to look at me. "Hans!" she scolded mildly. Then she went back to her carding. "You'll get over it," she added in a matter-of-fact tone, "just like your father did." She nodded her head and began rocking her chair for emphasis.

"Just like Father?" I objected. "He was tall."

"That's the way you remember him because you were smaller when he . . . when you saw him last. But now you're as tall as he was."

I was absolutely astonished. "You mean he was small?"

"Yes, in height, but not in other ways. In kindness, in strength and intelligence he was 10 feet tall. To most people he was a big man. You can be too, Hans. In height

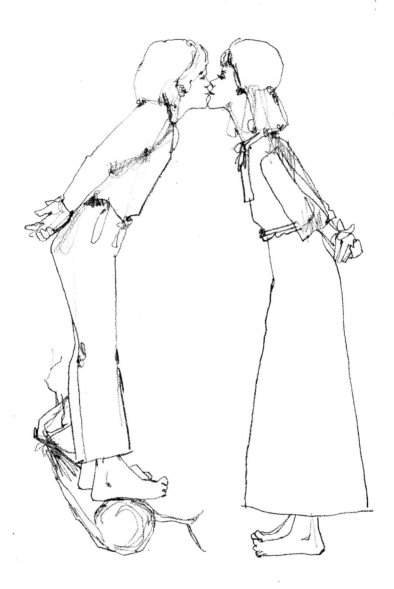

you're about as big as God planned, I guess, but as a man of God you can be real big."

I went on lamenting my size, especially when I thought about how much Sally Jo must have grown. But before long my problem seemed pretty small. On September 2 Atlanta fell. Now there seemed no stopping Sherman's army from coming our way.

Mother said, "If the Yankees do come this way we'll go back to Savannah. Maria and I will really have to depend on you and Klaus, Hans. You're the men of the family now."

Suddenly I felt 10 feet tall.

20. In the Eye of a Hurricane

For more than a month Sherman and his army perched in Atlanta like a horde of vultures trying to decide which bones in a burial mound to pick first. So our army circled north of Atlanta to destroy his supply lines.

President Davis quickly toured Georgia, assuring the citizens that Sherman would be forced into as disastrous a retreat from Atlanta as Napoleon had been from Moscow. He was so convincing that Mother started packing. And she traded some old family jewelry for two oxen and a wagon to replace our horses and old wagon that had long since been drafted by the army.

As it turned out, the trade was timely, because in mid-November we learned that instead of retreating Sherman was marching deeper into Georgia. Refugees reported that the Yankees had burned Atlanta, that "bluecoats" were now swarming the roads toward Augusta, carting off everything worth stealing and setting fire to whatever remained, and that in their scorched wake followed vast armies of runaway slaves.

Yet the rumors of Sherman's destination conflicted. Some said he was headed south toward Macon, others said southeast toward Charleston or even Savannah, but most said toward Milledgeville, from whence he would surely march on Augusta, which lay directly in the path of his ultimate destination — Richmond, Virginia.

Adding to our uncertainty, the newspapers printed desperate appeals from congress and the secretary of war in Richmond: "Georgians, hold fast. Obstruct the path of Sherman's army. Remove Negroes and cattle and food from his path. Strike him in flank and rear. Help is on the way to you." Then they printed glowing accounts of how Sherman's soldiers, faced with mass starvation, were surrendering by the thousands and how our tightening cordon around them would soon annihilate them.

Mother unpacked, then started packing again when eyewitnesses reported that the Yankees had captured Milledgeville, the state capital, with hardly a struggle.

Battalions of slaves began to build earthworks around Augusta. Old men and young boys rushed to man the defences, and that's when I changed my mind about leaving.

As I helped Mother pack I told her, "John Kraft has joined the militia. They'll need every one they can get!"

"A mere boy!" she answered.

"He's 16, same as I am. That's old enough."

"No, Hans. You're coming to Savannah with us!"

"But I'm needed here."

She placed Klaus's violin in the wagon, then looked at me intently. "No, and that ends it! They don't need you or anyone. It's all pointless. Pointless slaughter, and you're not going to be part of it."

"But, Mother . . . ." A strong hand gripped my shoulder. I looked back and saw Mr. von Rohr.

"Hans, I want to talk to you. Alone."

"Mother?" I said in a tone that begged her to say she couldn't spare me.

"Go ahead, Hans," she answered.

He led me through the house, out the back and down to the root cellar. Where was everyone — Klaus, Maria, Mrs. von Rohr, Carl, Tag, anyone? When I heard the cellar door close behind us, I looked about wildly for a weapon, any sort of weapon.

"Come along. I want to show you something." His arm around my shoulders gave me no choice. He drew me over to that high shelf, reached up, and removed several bottles. I glanced back, trying to see if I could reach the top of the stairs before he could stop me. He pulled out the revolver.

"Ever seen anything like this?"

"No, sir. Never!"

"I used to be pretty good with it. See, it's an army revolver. Given me by a Federal officer before the war."

I knew he was lying but said, "Yes, sir."

"I've kept it hidden away because of Carl. Little children and guns don't mix."

More lies. He knew I knew about the gun and was trying to cover up.

"I want you to have it. You're grown up now. Take it with you."

Trying to get rid of the evidence.

"Here." He handed it to me and I quickly pointed it at him.

"No, no, don't point it at anyone unless you have to. And don't tell your mother about it. Put it under your jacket. And listen, Hans, your mother needs you. I don't know what came between you and me, but remember — *she* needs you. She's still a very handsome woman, and if the Yankees get ahold of her . . . . Promise me you'll protect her. Will you do that? And no more of this militia nonsense?"

Even with the gun in hand, I was too scared not to promise.

The following morning on Broad Street we found several dozen wagons forming a train for the flight to Savannah. The von Rohrs came along to see us off, and Mother pleaded for them to come with us.

"This is our home and this is where we stay," Mr. von Rohr answered. "The Yankees can't frighten me away."

In his case, of course not, I thought to myself.

"Look," he said, "if you can't get through, come back. You're always welcome with us."

"Why shouldn't we get through?" Mother asked.

"Oh, no reason! Just another silly rumor. About Yankee cavalry heading toward Waynesboro to cut the city off from the south, but you know these rumors!"

Mother and Mrs. von Rohr were exchanging kisses when a small group of militia came marching by. Their sergeant, an ancient creature maybe 70 years old, stopped beside our wagon to study us.

"You!" he shouted at Klaus. "Where do you think you're going, and out of uniform?"

"He's never been in uniform," Mrs. von Rohr answered. He's only 17."

"Looks 18 to me," he growled. "A deserter for sure. You know I can have him shot?"

Mr. von Rohr assured the sergeant that Klaus was 17.

"That's old enough to fight, boy. C'mon. Form up with us. We're getting ready to meet the Yankees."

"No!" Mother protested loudly. "He's not a soldier. What does he know about fighting?"

"What do any of us know about fighting!" the sergeant answered in a very rude tone, pointing at the youths he was leading. Turning back to Klaus he barked, "You come along or I'll have my boys shoot you for a deserter."

"No!" Mother screamed. "You can't take him!"

"Dead or alive, Ma'am, we'll take him. Make up your mind."

She burst into tears.

"C'mon, boy. Time's a wasting!"

Klaus climbed down from the wagon. "No!" she cried, snatching at his shoulders. "The war's already killed my husband. Now you want to kill my son!"

"It's all right, Mother," Klaus said. "Do you want me to be less brave than Father?"

"Yes!" she cried with tears streaming down her cheeks.

"And be shot as a deserter?" Klaus countered.

She couldn't answer. Klaus reached up and caressed her hair. "God will take care," he told her.

"I'm coming too!" I volunteered.

"Then, form up!" the sergeant said and marched off with his hand on Klaus's elbow.

"Good-bye!" Klaus called to us.

Mr. von Rohr grabbed me as I was climbing down from the wagon. "No, Hans! You don't have to go, and you made a promise. Besides, you may meet the Yankees sooner than the militia. If you ever wanted to be a soldier, here's your chance, but with your mother!"

"Klaus!" Mother cried weakly, "Oh, Klaus!" Maria started to cry too.

Mother's stricken look made me stay, but my heart swelled with pride and of course envy as I watched Klaus march away. He had never wanted to be a soldier, and here he was going off to war like Father had while I was left behind!

Mr. von Rohr patted my jacket over the spot where I carried the revolver. "Remember, Hans, guard your mother and Maria. With your life if need be."

Our wagon train began to move, but Mother just stared teary-eyed off in the direction Klaus had taken, and mumbled, "My son, my son."

Once we were beyond sight of the city she grew silent and stayed that way throughout the morning and afternoon. Maria hung on to her much of the time; so except for Tag

I was left alone to plan what I'd do if the Yankees came, how I'd take command of the train and set up a defense that would defy every charge of those vandals.

The chilly, overcast sky was beginning to grow dark when we heard gunfire in the distance ahead. A lone rider came streaking up to our train yelling, "You all better turn back. Yankee cavalry's coming on through Waynesboro. General Wheeler's there giving 'em a scrap, but we can't hold 'em for long."

I managed to get our wagon turned around in the narrow road, but the panic shown by the other wagons didn't help. The gunfire grew steadily louder and closer. We had hardly got our wagons turned around when our cavalry came galloping past us, heading back toward Augusta.

"You better hurry too!" one of the troopers called. "Kilpatrick's bluecoats'll be hailing by soon enough!"

I urged our oxen on as fast as they would plod while our ragtag cavalry continued pouring past us in retreat. When the last of them faded from view, the darkening landscape looked utterly desolate. I pulled out the revolver, examined its chambers, then tucked it back in my belt.

Mother just stared absently off into the darkness, but Maria asked, "What's happening, Hans?"

"Well, Sis, seems we're going back to Augusta."

"Why?"

"There's Yankees back there in Waynesboro. We can't get through."

"Is that a Yankee chasing us?"

I looked back and saw a lone trooper coming from the direction of Waynesboro. He charged past us at full gallop. "No. He's one of ours, Maria, but the Yankees must be close behind."

The gunfire had ceased, and the stillness made the starless night seem all the more ominous. We plodded on for half an hour, always listening for the rumble of Yankee cavalry behind us.

"Hans, I hear hoofbeats!" Maria cried.

I did too, lots of them. "Lie down, Maria, Mother!" Mother sat motionless. "Mother!" I repeated. She didn't hear.

I pulled out the revolver and then I noticed something wrong about the hoofbeats. They weren't approaching us from behind but from the darkness ahead. In a few minutes our own cavalry passed us, heading back toward Waynesboro and looking more carefree than when they went by the first time.

"Is it the Yankees?" Maria whispered.

"No. Ours."

"Ours? I thought they ran off."

"Well, they're back, Sis. An officer's talking to the lead wagon now. He'll tell us what it's all about."

The train stopped as the officer came down the line to talk to each driver. At last he reined up by our wagon and explained that the Yankees were reportedly withdrawing from Waynesboro. If true, he'd dispatch a trooper to let us know.

So we waited, and ate our supper, then waited some more. Several hours had passed by the time a trooper came riding toward us yelling, "All clear. You all can turn around, but you better hurry. No telling about them dang Yankees. Might take a notion to return."

Whips cracked, drivers cursed, animals collided, and babies cried as several dozen wagons executed a frantic turn in the narrow road. Then we drove madly forward, with lots more cursing and crying. At last we entered Waynesboro. The streets were empty, but the smell of gunpowder still hung in the air. I cocked the revolver and searched for signs of Yankees behind every darkened building, tree, and bush. At the main intersection the road straight ahead led to Louisville and the Yankees. We took the left fork toward Millen, passed a small lake at the edge of town, then drove forward again at life-and-death speed.

Only when we had put a half dozen miles between us and Waynesboro did we break for the night. Even then I stood watch, gun in hand, for several hours before finally falling asleep.

The following day the cold, overcast sky filled me with foreboding. All day long we saw few signs of life. Even the prisoner-of-war camp at Millen was deserted.

On the third day the rolling land with its pleasant farms gave way to vast stretches of flat piney-woods country which, except for being cut here and there by abandoned rice plantations, was almost totally uninhabited. To some people in our train the country appeared eerie and to have about it the stillness of death, but to me it was a welcome sight because it was starting to look like home. I started to think about Sally Jo and Ned. I thought about Klaus too and wondered what he was doing now.

On the fourth day we entered Springfield and the world I had once known so well. We left the train and turned off toward the parsonage, going past many a familiar sight. Maria woke up and began to chatter like a magpie, as if she remembered much about Effingham County! Tag was alert and sniffed about as if he were remembering too. But Mother began to worry. What if the old parsonage was rented out?

We were relieved to find no one in it, but articles of furniture belonging to someone else cluttered the place. The beds, though, were without bedding or mattresses, and the stable was empty. Whoever had lived here had moved out — recently, it seemed, and in a hurry.

We waited till morning to unload the wagon. Afterwards I walked down the road toward the schoolhouse, hoping to see some familiar faces, one or two in particular. But I saw none, none at all. Suddenly it dawned on me that something was terribly wrong. Everything was deserted!

I continued down the road without seeing any sign of life until I neared a house by the school. There I saw a horse and wagon. A moment later a stranger dashed out of the house with a large sack over his shoulder.

"Where is everybody?" I called out.

"In Savannah! And you better be too if you don't want the Yankees to git you!"

"The Yankees? They're up Augusta way!"

"Don't know 'bout that, but they ain't no more than a long spit from this-a-way." With that he drove off as if he were going to a barn burning.

Mother had gone over to see the Wilkinses only to discover what I had. Tag and I walked up to Springfield to check at the county hall. Most of the people had left, but those I encountered confirmed the news that the Yankees were coming. So we repacked our wagon, and first thing the following day we set off for Savannah.

Outside the city, gangs of slaves were building an earthwork along a canal, and Confederate soldiers were manhandling artillery pieces into position.

"Is it true the Yankees are coming?" I called out.

"You'd better believe it!" a soldier replied. "But we'll give 'em what for!"

And here we thought we had escaped the storm. Instead we had been moving the whole time in the eye of a hurricane!

21. Bluecoat Storm

The only people in Savannah we knew well enough to stay with was Pastor Koenig's family, but Mother didn't want to impose on them. And since refugees already crowded Forsyth Park and the city squares, we camped our wagon in front of the old cemetery on South Broad Street. It was a good site. A water pump stood nearby, and the double line of moss-draped oaks which divided the spacious street along its entire length lent a sense of tranquility to our new home. We didn't have enough food to fully satisfy our hunger, but our first week's stay was peaceful enough. The following week, though, we heard the crackle of muskets and the report of cannons as the Yankees probed our defenses outside the city.

A one-legged veteran in a wagon not far from ours told me that Yankees now ringed Savannah on three sides but that the swamps and rivers surrounding most of the city were impassable to large armies and would force Sherman to attack from the only direction open to him—the west, where General Hardee was blocking his path with 20,000 soldiers and numerous cannons. Besides, for an all-out assault on the city Sherman would need fresh supplies from the Union fleet, and Fort McAllister prevented him from linking up with the fleet.

I figured the man knew what he was talking about. So when I wasn't hunting food, I calmly idled away the next few days carving little wooden soldiers and fantasizing myself leading attacks that hurled the bluecoat barbarians into watery graves.

Then came the news that Fort McAllister had fallen. The veteran told me, "We're in for it now!"

"Because of Fort McAllister?"

"That too, but Sherman is threatening to bombard the city if Hardee doesn't surrender. Before long this whole city'll be exploding. You better find shelter, son. When it comes, you sure won't want to be out in the open like this."

That afternoon he drove off in his wagon to who knows where. I didn't tell Mother why. Instead I took Maria inside the cemetery and said, "Sis, when the bombardment starts and if I'm not around, you bring Mamma in here." I showed her two ancient brick vaults about five feet high with only about a foot separating them. "You and Mother lie between these. They're strong and should shield you from almost anything."

She didn't thrill to the idea of taking refuge in a cemetery, especially at night, and the next day blabbed the whole thing. Mother's eyes teared up. To comfort her I said, "Would you feel better if we got across to South Carolina? Maybe I could build a raft or something."

"No, no," she sighed. "Klaus may be here. We can't leave."

"Klaus? Here? Why would he be here in Savannah?"

"I just feel it, and if he comes looking for us, we've got to be where he can find us."

"If he's here, I'll find him," I assured her.

In the days that followed I spent the daylight hours hunting for Klaus while Mother, Maria, and Tag hunted for food. They had no luck, so we were forced to eat only one meal a day.

As for finding Klaus, I quickly discovered how difficult this was. On the outskirts of the city soldiers abounded — some in grays, some in butternut homespuns, and some who couldn't be distinguished from ordinary citizens except that they wore a cartridge box and carried a rifle. "Do you know Klaus Schmidt?" I asked each group I met. And they usually shook their heads and hurried on. Some groups were too busy digging trenches or constructing sharp-pointed abatis even to answer. I spotted one motley-looking group without any semblance of uniform, and, figuring they must be with the militia, I asked them about Klaus.

"What outfit's he with?" a lanky one inquired.

"The militia."

"That's no help. So be we all."

Another just laughed. "Klaus Schmidt? With a name like that, what do you want to find him for?"

I wandered mile after mile without any success, but I did study the terrain and make some mental notes of how the Baron and I would dispose our forces for defense. Near dark, as I passed a stately brick house covered with ivy and surrounded by a high brick wall, I heard the strains of a familiar ballad coming from the back yard. I stopped to listen.

> A hundred months — 'twas flowery May,
> When up the hilly slope we climbed,
> To watch the dying of the day
> And hear the distant church bells chime.

Feeling that maybe someone here could help me, I entered through a bougainvillea arbor and saw five soldiers seated around a low fire. Their uniforms told me they were regulars but had come a long way and seen many a battle.

"You be the owner, boy?" one of them called, motioning with his head toward the chicken he was roasting.

"The owner?" I asked.

"Had to do it!" he apologized. "This here chicken were downright disloyal."

"Yeah!" said another. "Refused to take a oath of allegiance to Jeff Davis. Nothing for us excepting to execute him."

"Oh, it's not my chicken!" I assured them.

"Well, then, come set a spell and share our vittels."

They didn't know anything about Klaus, but since they were so friendly, and it was getting too dark to hunt further, I decided to accept their invitation.

Besides the chicken, we ate some rice soup flavored with rancid bacon, and I was just hungry enough to enjoy it. All five soldiers were from Kentucky and Tennessee. While they hunted lice under each other's roundabouts, they talked about their families and about Christmases of long ago. A boyish looking fellow, the only one without a straggly beard, made the deepest impression on me. He was from near Frankfort and was named Ken Daniels. Of his six brothers three were fighting for the Union and three for Dixie. He was the youngest of the boys, though he had two younger sisters. As he talked about home, I could feel the pain in his heart. Suddenly he grew silent, then just as suddenly began to sing in a soft and plaintive voice:

> Weeping, sad and lonely,
> Hopes and fears how vain!

The others joined in the remainder of the chorus:

> Yet praying, when this cruel war is over,
> Praying that we meet again!

They sat there under the stars in solemn silence. By the light of the fire's dying embers I could see they were a thousand miles away in thought, so I quietly rose, gave a small wave, and left.

After a night's sleep frequently interrupted by artillery fire, I packed my revolver under my coat and set out again to hunt for Klaus. Several blocks from where I had left off the night before, I found the whole landscape churned up. Many of the houses had gaping holes. Some had only a single wall left standing. Some were reduced to rubble. And tree after tree lifted only shattered limbs against the wintry sky.

I hurried on up the street hoping the reign of ruin would stop short of that stately house where I had met the five, but it didn't. The arbor was completely torn away, the trees splintered, and the walls of the house totally collapsed, except for one chimney that stood like a solitary mourner brooding over the smoldering debris.

In the back yard I found a gaping crater but no sign of the five. As I continued the search I wasn't really sure whether I was hunting for Klaus anymore or for those five. A mile or so up the road I came across the first signs of life — at first only stray soldiers, but then large groups digging trenches. Even here the signs of the night's bombardment were everywhere.

Then it came like the shriek of lost souls in hell! Without even thinking I threw myself to the ground and hugged it for dear life. A deafening explosion followed, and a house up the road spewed pieces of brick and lumber in every direction.

I got up and started to run. A terrifying howl passed overhead. I pasted myself against the earth. An instant later, a furious bang behind me. Again I got up to run. Another explosion hurled me to the ground. Then the air filled with screaming shells, and the whole world exploded — to the right and left, in front and behind. The ground retched, and trees and bricks went flying in all directions. A clump of earth hit me in the back. I turned over, only to see the sky raining wood and sand all around me. "Oh, God!" I screamed. I turned over and put my hands over the back of my head and prayed. Then I tried clawing into the hard-packed road until my fingers bled.

The racket was earsplitting, but between explosions I thought I heard someone. I forced myself to listen. Did I really hear someone? Yes, during the next interval I heard it again!

"Hans! Hey, is that you?"

"Yes!" I screamed, not daring to lift my head to look. A shell echoed my scream, and again the earth quaked beneath the blast.

"C'mon, boy. You oughtn't to be out there in weather like this!"

I lifted my head ever so slightly. I could see it. A hand waving just above a ditch. Then a blinding flash beyond the hand. The blast screamed in my ears and heaved me into the air. Something hit me with a real wallop.

Then came the voice again. "Crawl, boy! Crawl!"

The barrage sounded like a thousand thunder peals rolled into one and all bent on destroying me. I was paralyzed with fright, but my horror of being alone in this bombardment stirred me to movement. I slithered along the ground, stopped abruptly as another shell burst nearby, and instinctively tried to claw my way into the road. After some seconds I started crawling again. Forward and stop, for-

ward and stop, until at last a hand grabbed mine and dragged me into the ditch.

"Hey, it *is* Hans," someone said. I looked up into the bearded face of one of the five. "The Yankees sure are unsociable today, hey, Hans? And them being only guests!"

"And uninvited guests too!" a second added. The earth split beneath another blast, and we hugged the sides of the ditch like a long-lost love. It went on and on this way for I don't know how long. Then quite suddenly it stopped.

The silence transformed the world into a strangely unreal land — of the kind that exists only in a young child's imagination. After a minute I asked, "Is it over?"

"Never can tell," came the answer. "Them Yankees can be powerful ornery. Just let us 'uns relax a mite and they's back at it."

We peered over the lip of the ditch but saw little besides smoke. "Ha!" one of them quipped, "now that they's got their mortars heated up, I guess they's taken time out to cook some of our rice in 'em. Sure wish they'd learn another way to heat them there kettles!"

After a few minutes we stood up and that's when I noticed there were only four of them.

"Where's Ken?" I asked.

No answer. So I asked again.

"Up the road a mite," one of them finally said. "C'mon."

We stopped in front of what must have been a beautifully landscaped front yard. One of them told me, "They hit this place late last night, so we figured it was safe. But they sent another shot over this morning. I told you they was ornery!" He pointed past a small crater to a butternut uniform crumpled in a careless heap.

As we approached it I suddenly realized that someone was in the heap. I stopped. "Ken?" I asked with a sense of horror.

"Ken," came the reply.

One of the four walked over the rest of the way, kneeled down, and turned him face upward. He closed the lids over the staring eyes, then turned the boyish face sideways to expose the left temple. "It were so wee a hole! Hardly bigger than a flea bite," he said with broken voice. "So wee a hole!" He broke into tears, though he didn't make a sound.

I headed back toward our wagon, too torn up inside to look further for Klaus. Along my path lay bodies and parts of bodies. I clutched my stomach to keep from throwing up, then covered my ears to shut out the pathetic cries I was beginning to hear in the distance.

That night I lay awake, thinking of Ken, of his mother and little sisters who would wait in vain and all because of a wee hole, so wee a hole! And I wondered about his brothers in blue. The fuse that hurled that tiny piece of metal through his temple — could one of them have lit it?

I didn't tell Mother about my being caught in the bombardment, because if I did I knew she would forbid me to search any more. I wanted her to forbid me, but I also knew how much finding Klaus meant to her. Besides, if he was out there risking his life, could I do less? So in the morning I resumed the search.

The threatened bombardment of the city itself had not yet begun, but as I made my way to the front I kept close to the buildings, because when it did start I wanted to find shelter in a hurry. My search proved futile — that day and the next too, but at least no cannon shot fell within a mile of me.

On the night of the 20th hunger kept plaguing my sleep, so I sat up for some time thinking of how bleak our Christmas would be this year. When at last I fell asleep, a loud explosion woke me up. Huge fires from somewhere around the waterfront lit up the sky, and a number of people rushed by, headed in that direction.

"What's happening?" I called out.

"A boat blowed up or something," a man answered. "Someone said the cotton's on fire down there, and the guards is gone from the stores. C'mon and help yourself before the stuff's all gone!"

"But that's stealing. Don't you fear God, especially with the Yankees so near?"

"God? Long as Hardee's men guard us, what's to fear from God or the Yankees?" He hurried off after the others.

I slept later than usual that morning, but fires were still smoldering around the city as I set out once again to find Klaus. I had gone a dozen blocks when it struck me that I hadn't seen a single soldier. Always before there had been soldiers hurrying from place to place or just milling about the streets and squares. This time not a uniform anywhere. And I hadn't heard any of the usual sporadic rifle fire. Not a shot! Nor the sound of a single cannon.

Suddenly up the street I saw uniforms, lots of them, but all bluecoats! I rubbed my eyes. Yes, it was true! Bluecoats! In Savannah! I darted down a side street. Along the parallel street more bluecoats! I turned into an alley. Even more bluecoats! Every direction I turned it was raining bluecoats.

I sneaked through yards, climbed walls, and cut through alleys to make my way back to the wagon. When I told Mother the news, she didn't bat an eyelash. "Maybe the war's over," she said with a sigh of relief.

Where were all our soldiers, I wondered. Why weren't they appearing suddenly in every window and alley, firing at the Yankees?

Several citizens stood in their doorways weeping as a wild-looking man walked by carrying a sign that said Repent!" He called out at the top of his lungs: "Woe to them that trust in chariots because they are many but do not look unto the Holy One of Israel, neither seek the Lord!"

22. Guerilla Warfare

A wire stretched across Bay Street from the City Exchange to the Customs House. From it hung a huge American flag, under which endless ranks of blue-clad soldiers marched to the martial strains of a Union band. We learned that General Hardee's men had evacuated the city during the night, escaping into South Carolina by a bridge hastily constructed over rice barges, and that the mayor had gone out during the morning to surrender the city to Sherman.

Across the street from where I stood General Sherman sat stiff in his saddle taking the salute of his victorious vandals. "One well-aimed bullet," I thought, "and we'd be rid of this Sherman." But while some people wept, others, especially of the merchant class, smiled and joked. A few even cheered, as if glad their shops had been spared and they could again carry on business as usual. I couldn't understand this. The Yankees were our enemies whom it was our duty to fight in whatever way we could.

For the present, though, I had to devote myself to the struggle of keeping our family alive. We were completely out of food. What little currency Mother had saved was worthless, since only Federal money would now be honored. To make matters worse, the weather turned unusually cold, chilling us to the bone, and we had no wood for a fire. Mother came down with a severe chest cold and her face became gaunt, her eye sockets hollow.

Our oxen also were suffering. In a moment of desperation I even thought of letting them graze in the cemetery, but Yankee officers, to whom nothing seemed sacred, beat me to it and stabled their horses there.

Our situation was such that in spite of Mother's pride I went to seek help from Pastor Koenig. I found Yankee officers quartered in his house. They said they knew nothing at all of his whereabouts, but one of his neighbors told me he had left six months earlier to seek other employment since church attendance had fallen off and inflation had eaten up his meager salary.

What now? The Yankees promised to feed the population but said they must first cut a new channel through the barricaded river. Meanwhile our oxen would die, and so would we unless I could do something.

An idea struck me, to which Mother agreed. We drove our wagon over to Wright Square where a cattle auction was held each month. I figured maybe we could barter an ox for some food, fodder, and wood. But we found the square filled with Yankee soldiers building makeshift huts for themselves. Next, we tried the market at Ellis Square. I haggled with a number of merchants but none were interested. I approached customers, but they brushed me aside. I tried Union soldiers, and they laughed at the scrawny condition of our oxen. A planter seemed interested but not interested enough to give me what I was asking for.

"How long do you think that fugitive from a boneyard will last?" he asked. "And I'd have to feed it good fodder. Heaven knows the Yankees ain't left me much of that either."

So I was forced to sell on his terms: five pounds of rice, a dozen raccoon oysters, a bushel of fodder, and enough corn and wheat for a spring planting. No wood, though, and this was bad because the Yankees were sacking every house in the city for wood. Later a Yankee trooper offered me a bundle of wood and an axe for Klaus's violin. An outrageous offer, but I accepted.

Christmas Eve was heralded in by the pealing of church bells — at least, those bells that had not been melted down long ago to make cannons. As their brassy tones echoed in the chilly night air, we gathered around our Christmas fire. We had neither house nor hearth, tree nor gifts. Yet the moon bathed the city in silvery light that made it seem like Christmas in spite of all.

On Christmas morning we walked to the nearest church but found it closed. We walked further and were amazed to discover how many churches no longer held services. The First Baptist Church was open, though, so we attended there.

Afterwards when we returned to our wagon-home I got out my bag of marbles and recalled the Christmas Father had given them to me. How lucky we were then! Then I got to wondering about Klaus and about Ken's four comrades. How were they spending Christmas? Plowing through a rice field or felling trees or lying in the cold mud to escape some screaming shells? Or maybe lying in a heap in some God-forsaken swamp, unburied? I thought, "How lucky we are even now — Mother, Maria, and I!"

The weather warmed up for several days, then turned cold again. Our firewood was already gone, so I chopped up the chairs in the wagon and used this to cook our rice with. Tag seemed to make out all right, scavenging among the bluecoats, but not so the rest of us. So when we heard that General Sherman had arranged with the mayor to let citizens leave by boat under a flag of truce for either Augusta or Charleston, I asked Mother if we should go.

"No, not to Charleston or Augusta," she said. "Klaus wouldn't know where to find us. But we can move back to the parsonage."

Early the next day we left the city, and none too soon. We had heard that there was an outbreak of typhus among the soldiers, and the place was beginning to look like a pest hole, with dead Yankee horses littering the streets. But outside the city the devastation was absolutely unbelievable. The charred ruins of plantation after plantation lined the road. The Mulberry Grove plantation, once the property of Nathaniel Greene, was gone — its manor house, its fields, its stately groves of mulberry trees, all nothing but an ash heap.

Further along we saw the vast improvised camps of the slaves who had traveled hundreds of miles in Sherman's wake. As a Union officer rode by, a loud cheer rent the air. I realized then that not everyone in the South viewed the war as I did. To these slaves the Yankees were liberators.

Here and there along our route a decrepit house of some impoverished planter had escaped the Yankees' wrath, almost as if Sherman's hordes had reserved their flaming vengeance for the wealthy while taking pity on the poor. This gave me hope that maybe our house had been spared.

Since Effingham County had few wealthy plantations, the devastation there wasn't quite as thorough. The parsonage had been spared the torch, but the rail fence had apparently been used for fire wood as had the posts that once supported the porch roof, which now sagged crazily, almost blocking the front door. The shutters on all windows had been torn away too, probably for fire wood. Not a stick of furniture remained in the house or a jar of food in the storeroom. The church, I later discovered, was badly burned, and only a providential rain had kept it from being utterly gutted.

The weather continued cold and Mother's cough grew worse. By New Year's Day we had enough rice left for one more meal, and the few neighbors who had returned to their homes were in just as bad a way.

Shortly before noon Simeon, Miss Julia, Mrs. Mahlstedt, and several other members came in a group to see us. For a while we stood around exchanging news. Mrs. Mahlstedt's husband had recovered from his wound at Manassas only to be killed later at Chancellorsville. No one knew what had become of the Hansers. Simeon was now living in their house. Pastor Dorow had left a year earlier to seek other employment—for the same reasons as Pastor Koenig in Savannah. An invading enemy had once again used Jerusalem Church over by the landing as a stable for its horses. Though not burned, the church would take a long time to fix up.

When the conversation began to lag, I got up the nerve to ask about Sally Jo.

"Oh, the Klugs got away well ahead of the Yankees!" Mrs. Mahlstedt told me. "Went to South Carolina. Somewhere near Columbia, I think."

That was that! "Do you know anything about Ned, who lived up near Ebenezer?" I asked.

Simeon spoke up, "Yessir. His family, they stayed right there, and the Yankees treated them right proper."

"And Ned?"

"Well, he done got hisself in the navy. And they put him on the *Atlanta*. That's a ironclad, and, well, it started mixing it up with the Yankees, and from what I heard folks tell, well, it run aground and was captured. So I reckon that there boy is a stuffing hisself in a Yankee prison camp, living high on the hog."

"Oh!" I said and kneeled down to rub Tag's ears. The way he looked at me, I think he was remembering too.

Mrs. Mahlstedt spoke up. "One of the reasons we came by this morning was, well, because it's Sunday and we haven't had church in a long time. We were wondering if maybe Hans could lead us in worship—you know, a few hymns and prayers and maybe a Bible reading?"

I felt a bit foolish but what could I say? The job I did wasn't as good as Father could have done, but the people seemed appreciative, and I actually enjoyed the experience.

After the service Simeon said, "We'd better do some fixing on that there porch. I can have it fixed in a jiffy and won't need no nails neither. But first we all needs some vittels in our innards. You all got some food?"

Mother said, "We've got a handful of rice but that's all." The others remained silent.

"Well, I has a little," he continued. "The Yankees didn't

take mine. Even gave me some. Not much, but I'll share it with you all."

Miss Julia fiddled with her bonnet a second, then said, "I have a little food they didn't find." Then others offered to share what they had hidden. So those of us near starvation received food. That night I thanked God for the generosity of His people!

The amount of food we received wasn't much, so I made up my mind to guard it with my life, especially our planting seed. Mrs. Mahlstedt had warned me to hide it well. "If the Yankees come back, they'll tear your house apart to find it," she told me.

I supplemented our meager diet with some fish from the river, but later in the month the river began to flood, and from then on I came back empty-handed more often than not. Once again our situation was growing desperate. Our house was bare, our patched clothes were turning to drafty rags, and our food supply couldn't last the winter even with the most stringent rationing.

The one thing we had in abundance was a source for wood. Since Mother and Maria were over visiting with Miss Julia, I grabbed the axe and called to Tag. "Come on, boy, let's go chop us up a few trees."

On my way out the kitchen door I spotted a Yankee soldier sauntering around the bend just beyond the stable. He wore his cap tipped cockily to one side and sang merrily as the holster on his belt and the half-empty sack slung over his shoulder swung to and fro.

"No Yankee's going to get our food," I told Tag and raced in the back door to get the revolver from my bedroom. Then I ran into the parlor and peered out the window. He was coming up to the house! Tag's nostrils swelled, his snout wrinkled.

"Shh!" I said and tiptoed through the hallway and out the back door toward the kitchen house, with Tag at my heels. "He better not come through that door!" I warned.

He knocked. "Hey! Anybody home?"

The laundry hanging out in the yard gave it away that our house was lived in. "Anybody home?" he called again.

I heard the doorknob turn, so I raced into the kitchen and on into the storeroom, from where I could see if he came through the house to the back door. Tag was so excited I had difficulty keeping him quiet.

The back door swung open. "Hey, anyone home?" The soldier stepped out into the yard. I spun around and aimed the revolver at the kitchen door.

He knocked on it.

"Don't you come in!" I silently warned and pulled back the hammer. My hands trembled. The door opened, and Tag growled. The blue uniform and cocky cap stepped into the doorway. "Hey, any . . . ."

"Bam!" Flame and smoke belched from the barrel. He gripped his chest, his eyeballs bulging at me with surprise. He slowly spun around backwards and fell outside, out of view.

The gun shook loose from my trembling hand. I felt sick and stunned by what I had done. Tag ran to the doorway and stood there barking.

I forced myself over to the doorway but couldn't look down at the man I had just shot. "What would the Baron say!" I scolded myself. "This is part of being a soldier." I opened my eyes and looked and almost threw up.

I stepped around his body, then ran over to the stable. I racked my brain as my body convulsed. Mother mustn't know. The Yankees will come looking for him. Had to get rid of the body. But where? Under the trees! No. May damage the roots and kill the trees — a telltale clue. Over in our field! No. Somebody might see me dragging him over there or digging the grave. Here in the stable! Of course! I could dig in here and no one would see me.

I worked in a frenzy, but with only an axe and hands to dig with the going was slow. Down a foot the ground

turned rather sandy. The digging speeded up. Two feet. Three feet. Deep enough! I fetched a blanket from my bedroom, threw it over the soldier so I wouldn't have to look at him, then dragged him over to the stable, and threw up.

Once I had him and his sack buried I spread the excess dirt all around the stable floor and covered it with what hay was still up in the loft. With the axe I plowed up and turned over the blood-covered ground by the kitchen steps, stomped it back down again, then hid the revolver in the hayloft. Then I waited for Mother and heaved up another precious meal.

"Hans looks sick, Mamma," Maria said when they came home.

"No wonder. He must be starved! Look, Hans, Simeon caught us a turtle. We'll have a good soup tonight." I almost brought up a meal I didn't know I had.

Later, as I fetched water from the well, Mother gathered some wood from the pile next to the stable. She returned to the kitchen without noticing anything amiss. So far, so good! But I wondered if it would be that easy with those thorough Yankees.

23. Yankee, Go Home!

Late in January I heard horses and wagons going by on the Augusta road till I thought there'd be no end of them. I went over to see what was happening. Half of Sherman's army was rumbling north to cross the flooded Savannah for an invasion of South Carolina.

I thought now that the Yankees were leaving, maybe everything would turn out all right after all. Maybe I'd even be able to go into the stable again without getting sick.

So I skipped all the way back to the house to see what I could do for Mother.

Earlier in the month Mother had shown her ingenuity by making mattresses out of pine needles and wagon canvass so we wouldn't have to sleep on hard board floors anymore. I had traded the wagon for a small bucket of nails, a hammer, and a saw. With lumber salvaged from a few burned-out houses I built a table, benches, and three beds. Just in time too, because Mother's cough had grown so severe that we had to confine her to bed.

I found her being spoon-fed some broth by Maria, who had become the regular mistress of the house, taking care of Mother, cooking what little there was to cook, and washing our clothes — without soap, of course, since none was to be had.

"How's the cough?" I asked.

"The same," Mother answered.

"Can I fix you a fresh plaster?"

"No, no! One's enough for a day. For a lifetime too."

I suspected that Mother had pneumonia, but the doctor in Springfield had been drafted two years earlier; so we had to depend on Miss Julia's book of home remedies. On the basis of this, Miss Julia had mixed up some sort of turpentine plaster which didn't seem to do a thing for the cough, but it sure blistered the chest.

I went out to fashion a wooden plow. In a short time Maria came out to fetch some water. She was bubbling over with excitement.

"You'll never guess, Hans, but you know what Miss Julia told me this morning about Mr. Hildebrandt, your old schoolteacher? Well, after we left, he raised the tuition so high that he lost most of his students and then he didn't have enough left. So they drafted him into the army, but he argued and argued. Well, they took him anyway. But guess what? He talked them into giving him garrison duty at Fort Jackson, and, well, but he didn't stay there. He

talked them into a new job. Guess what kind? He got himself made overseer of some slaves they drafted to dig
trenches around Savannah. Can you imagine that? Him
a slave driver, I mean?"

"Quite well, yes!"

"But oh, Hans . . . ." Her face turned grave. "I heard
about your friend too! What's his name? Ned?"

"About Ned?"

"They heard the other day." She picked up the kettle
and carried it into the kitchen.

"Heard what, Maria?" I asked, chasing after her.

She hung the kettle over the fire, then turned toward me
but with her eyes on the floor. "I'm sorry, Hans. He's dead.
Died in the prison camp. From typhus, they said."

I felt stunned, for a split second because of the news
but then because I didn't feel anything. Why didn't I feel
anything? Had too many years gone by? Had the war with
all its separations and deaths made me callous? Was I just
getting too old for tears? Or had my killing someone turned
me cold and indifferent?

I found Tag under the kitchen steps and took him with
me for a walk to the schoolhouse. At the fork in the road
I saw Sally Jo, book in hand, coming toward me. Just for
a moment I saw her. So clearly. But not Ned. As I entered
the schoolyard I smelled coffee, then saw Mr. Hildebrandt's malevolent mustache. Why that buzzard and not
Ned?

The schoolhouse looked smaller now. The door was
boarded up and the exterior walls needed paint badly.
I slowly pivoted, taking in the whole scene—the schoolhouse, the brooding pine forest that surrounded the school-
yard, the woodpile where Sam and his pals liked to sit,
the field where they marched. Faces flitted by. Sam's,
Bob's, Klaus's, almost everyone's. For just a second
I thought I even heard their voices. But not Ned's. Why
not Ned's?

Out by the road I nearly bumped into a Negro boy who looked vaguely familiar, like the boy from the plantation down the road who used to wait for us outside the school.

"Johnny?" I asked.

He leaned down to pet Tag. "That Ned's dog, Hans?"

"Yes. It was."

He stood up and said defiantly, "I'll go to school here!"

"Oh?" I said, knowing that Negroes had never been allowed in the school before.

"I'm free now! So I can learn books like white folk. And someday I'll live in a plantation house."

I took another look at the school, hoping to see Ned's face or to feel something about him, then asked rather absently, "Do you still live on the plantation?"

"No, I has a nice house now!"

"Where?"

"Want to see?"

Why couldn't I see Ned? It was as if he had never been, as if Tag had always been mine and that river pirate had been only a figment of my imagination.

"Want to see?" he repeated.

"Yes, that's what I came for."

He looked at me quizzically. "You did?"

"Oh, I'm sorry! You were saying?"

"I was saying if you want to see my house, come on."

As he led me through the pines he talked a lot about the Yankees and glowed every time he mentioned them.

Though not interested in this excursion, I commented, "You must be glad they came."

He eyed me suspiciously, as if making up his mind whether or not to reveal his feelings. Then a defiant look came over him, and he said, "Yes! They's our saviors!"

"Well, I'm glad you're free and can go to school now."

At the end of the forest we came to a swamp devoid of trees except for one majestic pine that stood on a high spot about 100 feet out. Near the tree leaned a little shack, made out of all sorts of odds and ends, that one stiff breeze would easily topple. Johnny led me over the narrow causeway that connected the forest to this swamp island.

"This is where I lives now," he said proudly.

"That's a *nice* house?" I blurted out. "Surely the old huts on the rice plantations are better than that!"

"But it's *mine!*" he answered. "And the land is mine. No one can take it away from me or me from it."

"Do you have food?" I asked.

"A mite, but the Yankees is bringing us some more today. They brung us blankets too."

He invited me into his house and introduced me to his mother and two little sisters, about two and three years old. Though I felt like an intruder, his mother immediately set a plate on the box at one end of the room and said, "Have some food with us."

"Thank you, ma'am, but no. As it is, you won't have enough for yourselves." She insisted with such sincerity that I sat on the floor before the grits she spooned out and began to eat.

Four piles of pine needles — the family's beds — covered the floor in the other half of the room. Along the side wall several piled-up boxes served as cupboards. These apparently held all the family's possessions. It was obvious the family did all its cooking outside and had no way to heat the house, because one spark would set the shack off like a match. The only light inside came from the open doorway. Yet to Johnny this hovel was a palace because it was his and he was free.

As I ate, Johnny talked about life under bondage and how different things would be when the Yankees finished with the war and could get around to helping all the freed slaves. They would give them good farming lands and fine schools. So when he was old enough, he was going to join the Yankee army to help end the war. His mother frequently nodded her agreement.

I was just downing my last mouthful when in barged a Yankee soldier, built like a bull and wearing sergeant's stripes. The grits stuck in my throat.

There was no way to escape. I was trapped. What made them think of the stable? I thought sure they wouldn't look for the body there.

"Here's your rice," the sergeant said, thrusting a small sack at Johnny. I gulped and the grits went down.

"What about the other sack?" his mother asked. "We's to get two. That's what they told us."

The sergeant peered over his shoulder at her. "The second sack," he said holding it aloft, "is for you if you can pay."

"But we don't got no money."

"You must have something I can use — whiskey, a gold ring. You must've stole something." He looked around the barren shack. For the first time apparently he noticed me. "What you doing here?"

"Visiting," I said with nervous relief.

"That's bad business, mixing with these darkies. I don't like it, not at all! Why don't you run along home?"

"But aren't they your friends? You fought to set them free."

"To set them free?" he sneered. "Not on your tintype! I fought for the Union. For all I care these darkies can starve. Or ship 'em back to Africa! I bring 'em food because I carry out orders. Otherwise . . . ."

Johnny's face contorted the way it might if he had just been stabbed by his best friend.

"Well, I see you got nothing here," the sergeant continued, "so I'll just keep this here sack."

He started to leave, but catching a longer glance at the mother, he stopped in the doorway and called out, "Hey, boy! Come in here!" A tall Negro walked in, wearing a Yankee uniform. "Boy," said the sergeant, "why don't you take up with this woman here? Looks like she could use a man around the place."

"Desert the army, Sarge?" the soldier asked. "Why do you tell me to do a thing like that?"

"Because I don't want you niggers moving up north on us when the war's over!"

The soldier merely hung his head, but Johnny thrust the sack of rice at the sergeant. "Here! We won't eat your food!"

The sergeant's eyes narrowed. He slammed the sacks onto the floor and growled, "You'll eat it if I tell you to!"

"No! I'm free. You can't tell me what to do."

The sergeant drew himself up to his full height and his whole frame heaved. "I can and I will!" Then his words began slowly and softly but grew louder until the last was a scream: "You eat it, hulls and all, here and NOW!"

Johnny didn't budge, but Tag whimpered and the children began to cry.

The sergeant suddenly grinned, almost as if the whole thing had been a joke. With great calm he struck a match on his belt, held it over the pine-needle beds, and whispered between his teeth, "Eat it or this place goes up in smoke!"

Johnny stood firm. The sergeant dropped the match on the pine-needles, and his grin grew. Johnny rushed forward to put out the flame, but the sergeant easily shoved him back and stood blocking his path. Tag grew bold and grabbed the sergeant's pant leg. The sergeant kicked him away and yelled, "Keep that dog back or you won't have one!" So I held Tag back.

Once the fire was going good, the sergeant picked up the two rice sacks and walked out triumphantly. A few moments later the flames forced the rest of us to abandon the house.

As the two soldiers disappeared into the woods at the other end of the causeway, Johnny shouted, "Some saviors!"

"Yankees!" I said in agreement.

"That's right, Yankee, go home!" his mother cried as she huddled her frightened girls in her arms.

I felt a lump in my throat. And my eyes turned misty. I was on the verge of crying and wanted to but couldn't quite.

I took Johnny's family along to stay at our house until he and I could build a new house with whatever lumber we could salvage from some of the deserted ruins.

As we walked, the lump in my throat persisted. So did the mist in my eyes. Suddenly, as we passed the schoolhouse, through the mist I saw Ned racing toward me and I heard Klaus beside me yelling, "Hurry up, Ned, or you'll be late again!"

"Don't you all fret. If I git in a fix with Mr. Hildebrandt, the Baron'll show me how to escape. Ain't that so, Hans?"

My tears dissolved him. I bent down and hugged Tag. "You old pirate!" I cried. Then I couldn't stop crying.

"There, there," Johnny's mother said, "everything's going to be all right. You'll see."

"Yes," I sobbed, trying to block the welcome flood with my sleeve, "everything'll be all right now." And I hugged her two little girls and wetted their cheeks.

24. Momentous April

With Simeon's help we completed Johnny's new house in just eight days. Simeon brought over a large turtle for the celebration and was showing it to us when three Yankee soldiers in a wagon stopped in front of our house.

I started to run toward the stable to get the revolver, but Simeon grabbed me.

"Steady, boy. No needs to carry on like that," he said out of the side of his mouth. "I think they means to give you all some vittels."

He was right. They gave us flour, rice, salt, a rooster and a hen, and gave the same to Johnny's family. Johnny started to refuse it but his mother hushed him up.

After they had unloaded the goods, one of the soldiers asked, "You folks happen to see a young soldier around here several weeks back?"

"Thousands of them," Johnny said. "They went north!"

"No, I mean just one. He was on foot and carrying a large sack . . . ."

"No, sir!" I said. The others agreed.

"Well, he headed up this way all by himself. Happy-go-lucky kid. He knew we'd be bringing food out this way soon, but Sammy — that's his name — he couldn't wait. Said folks around here might starve before the army got around to passing out food. Collected some on his own and set off to pass it out. At least, that's what he said. Hard to believe he was just deserting. Seemed too fine a boy for that. Well, shows you never can tell! Five men in our outfit down with typhus, and now a deserter!"

"He was passing out food?" I asked.

"Yep, so he said. Well, I guess they'll be through here before long hunting for him. For some other deserters too."

A week later the Federal Government in Savannah ordered all civilians to surrender their fire arms. I didn't surrender my revolver because the night of the food delivery, amid many anguished prayers for forgiveness, I gave it its proper burial in our outhouse.

I didn't know what to think anymore. In the beginning I hadn't thought about the causes or issues of the war, only the excitement. And now, just when I had begun to see there was an issue, it dissolved before my eyes. Was the war to free the slaves or not? Were those in blue uniforms our enemies or not? More and more I began to wonder if the real enemy — to black and white, to those in blue and those in gray — wasn't the war itself.

The war kept taking its toll on us in different ways. Miss Julia showed me a copy of the Savannah *Republican* which showed clearly that supplies were arriving from the North in abundance. One retail druggist had an ad listing Mrs. Winslow's Soothing Syrup, Busband's Magnesia, Keyser's Salve, and Drake's Bitters. They were there waiting to be purchased for "moderate prices," but the war had left us penniless, and we couldn't get Mother so much as a small bottle of molasses or honey for her cough.

Then too we had constant bouts with hunger. A few generous neighbors, especially Simeon, stood again and again between us and starvation. Occasionally the Yankees passed out some food, but anytime one of them came near our house, my skin just crawled, no matter how many times I checked the stable to make sure I hadn't left any clues.

Our clothing situation was even more serious. We were down to the clothes on our backs. The rest were rags. If we had had needle and thread, Maria could have mended them. As it was, she painstakingly pulled some rags apart thread by thread for eventual use if and when we could get a needle. Some rags she wrapped around her feet because she had outgrown what had remained of her shoes. The rest of the rags I was making into a harness for the ox to pull the plow by when it came time for the spring planting. I had doubts, though, whether these rags would hold.

One chilly March evening as I prepared for bed, Maria knocked on my door. "Hans, better let me have your clothes. I'll wash them and get them hung out so they'll be dry by morning."

"Come in, Maria. I want to talk to you about that."

"You don't want me to do them at night?"

"No, that's fine. Can't have us running around like jay-birds in the daytime."

"Oh, Hans! I always have my coat on when I'm doing my dress."

"Yes, well, it's the way you do your dress, and Mamma's and my stuff. We've got to make them last."

"I know that, Hans."

"So better take it easy on them. No pounding them or twisting them."

"I don't do that anymore. Just boil them."

"Better cut that out too. Just soak them in cold water."

"They'll never get clean that way."

"They don't anyhow, not without soap. What do you want — boiled clothes or no clothes?"

Maria gave in; so besides few clothes we had dirtier clothes.

Thus the winter passed.

With the onset of spring I tried my hand at plowing. The rag harness tore the first day. I took out the offending link and tried again. The harness tore in another place. For three days I plowed and patched, plowed and patched till I didn't have enough left to patch with. And if I didn't get the plowing done, we wouldn't survive six months. I laid the harness aside in disgust and went over to the river to catch some fish.

I caught three and proudly presented them to Mother, who was up and well again.

"And I have something for you," she said. "The Yankees were by again . . . ."

I ran over to the window and looked out at the stable.

"Hans, what *is* the matter with you? They're not here now. But they brought us some blankets. Said they're moving one of their hospitals. And for you . . . ." She went to the house and returned with a blue roundabout. "It's just your size."

"Mother, you expect me to wear a Yankee uniform?"

"Well, you always did want to wear a blue uniform."

"But not a Yankee one! I'd go back to those rags on the harness first!"

"Why don't you use it for the harness?" Maria said with a wisdom beyond her years. And that's exactly what I did. It proved singularly successful, so I began making good progress with the plowing and felt thankful for the Yankee donation—at least at first, until we discovered we had lice.

"The Yankees weren't content to give us just their blankets." I told Mother. "They had to give us their vermin."

"Well, we'll boil the blankets. We'll have to boil our clothes too."

I agreed but asked, "What do we do about our coats? We can't boil them."

"We'll conduct a louse hunt in them."

Which we did, only it wasn't quite so easy. Just when we thought we had them all, one would find its way out of a frayed sleeve or a hole in the lining.

"We'll never get all the filthy beasts!" I told Mother. "And they've probably got a million eggs in there too."

"Well, we've seen just about the last of the cold weather for a while. Soon we can boil them."

"But they'll be no good then."

"If they're not, they're not."

"And what about next winter?" I protested.

"By then, who knows! We may have chickens to sell, and eggs, maybe even some corn."

So on the few chilly evenings remaining we donned our pestiferous outer garments and surrendered some blood to the unvanquished vermin that the Yankees had bequeathed us.

April came, and except for the Yankee patrols that continued to snoop and pry, all seemed well with the world. The azaleas in front of the house were blooming, our hen had hatched some chicks, the planting was done, and only one or two mornings were chilly enough to make us wear our coats and serve up a few free meals to our uninvited guests.

On the 10th of the month, though, we heard that Lee had surrendered to Grant in Virginia. Mother was elated because it meant the war would soon be over and Klaus could return. I felt as if the Baron had just surrendered, and I was in a foul mood until it occurred to me that the last of those snooping Yankees might be going home now too.

Mother celebrated by making plans to decorate the kitchen for the Easter service the following Sunday. The handful of the faithful would be over then for me to conduct their Sunday morning service as usual. As I prepared for that, she told me, "From now on you read our family devotions too. You're the man of the house. Oh, and give me your coat! We'll count this morning as our last donation for the support of aged lice." She went about boiling the coats with a cheer I had not seen since the day we heard about Father.

For the next several days I raided ruined houses for lumber and made benches for the parlor so we could hold the Easter service there. Mother had come down with a fever and headache, and had taken to bed, but Maria took care of her plans for the decorations.

"Hans, you know what Sunday is?" she asked while fashioning a crude flower pot.

"Sure, dummy. Easter."

"It's your birthday too. If you'll get me a corncob I'll make you a present."

"What could you make for me?" I laughed.

"A pipe. You're going to be an old man now. Seventeen. And all old men should have a pipe!"

"And all young brats a spank on their bottom! Mind you, be careful. I'm the man of the house now. So off to bed with you."

In the morning I went out to the kitchen for a rice breakfast, but no rice was cooked and Maria wasn't about. I went to her room and found her in bed. "Ah," I said, "and see how young brats treat aging people? Sleeping in and letting me perish of hunger! And us with a mother down sick!"

"Hans, don't tease. I ache all over and my head hurts and I feel like I'm burning up."

I felt her head. She was burning up. "Well, looks like I'm the cook now, huh? You just stay put, and if I don't burn the water, I'll get you some breakfast."

"I'm not hungry, Hans. Just get me some water. I'm so thirsty. And maybe you can make Mamma some breakfast."

Mother had no appetite either, but between her and Maria they kept me running almost constantly for water. Mother did want me to read the Bible to her, though. "Isn't fitting," she told, "even when you're sick to miss reading the Bible on Good Friday."

I thought their fever would let up by Saturday, but it didn't. Neither did the aches in their joints, nor their headaches. I went out to the well to get them some water. Mr. Wilkins rode by and called out, "Hear the news? President Lincoln's been assassinated!"

"Seen Miss Julia around?" I called back.

"Nope. Not today."

"Well, if you do, tell her I need her doctor book."

"All right. But ain't that welcome news about old Abe?"

"I guess, but a doctor'd be more welcome right now." But thanks to the war, none was to be had.

Easter morning the faithful gathered in our undecorated parlor. After the brief service they went to wish the family a happy Easter. Maria thanked them, and as they left her room, she asked me to stay.

"I'm sorry, Hans. I mean about your birthday and all. I really was going to make you something."

I gave her a kiss on her burning cheek. "I know, but there's only one present I really want. Just get well, please?" She tried to smile.

Mother seemed improved. She was still feverish but said her headache was practically gone, and she chatted with the visitors.

"Say," Miss Julia said, "there's your trouble. You got a rash on your arm."

We all looked and saw tiny, dark red spots. In some places she looked like she was bleeding under the skin. Mother said, "They're on my side and stomach too. I guess that fish Hans caught the other day didn't agree with me."

"I don't know, Miss Schmidt," Simeon said shaking his head. "Looks more like cabin fever to me."

"Cabin fever?" Miss Julia asked. "What's that?"

"Well, that's what they calls it. I seen black folk get spots like that down on the rice plantation. 'Tain't nothing to go messing with. We all better git you some good doctoring or something."

"Simeon, you worry too much," Mother said.

"Just the same, you better look it up in your book, Miss Julia."

"I'll do that for certain soon as I get home. Hans, you should've told us sooner. Trying to carry on by yourself!"

Mrs. Mahlstedt agreed. "Sick folk need a woman's touch. But we'll help out till your mother and Maria are back on their feet."

After they all left, Mother told me, "You let them help, Hans. Goodness knows you've got enough else to do." She gulped down a glass of water and said, "I've been meaning to talk to you, and this being your 17th birthday, I guess it's about time. I don't know whether Klaus is coming back or not . . . ."

"He'll be coming home real soon, you'll see."

"Well, I've prayed hard enough for that. If it's God's

will. Remember that, Hans, always if it's God's gracious will. He knows best what's good for us."

"Yes, ma'am."

"You know, Hans, your father always felt it was God's will that you be a pastor someday."

She stopped as if growing very tired, so I said, "I know, but maybe he was wrong."

"Maybe. Maybe. But I pray that he was right, because that's what I want you to be too. You'd be a good one, Hans."

I looked out the window at the stable. "Oh, Mother, you don't know! If you did . . . ."

"I'm thirsty, Hans, and tired. Get me the drink, please." I picked up the glass and started for the door. "Think about it, Hans. Just think . . . ." Her head fell to the pillow as if exhausted by all the talk.

Miss Julia didn't find anything in her book about cabin fever, which was a relief to me, because any disease not written up in a doctor's book obviously could not be all that serious. Except that the fever wouldn't let up. Maria broke out in the rash too.

Tuesday Mother became delirious. She mumbled about Klaus, about Maria, even about Father's joining the army. When she came out of it, Miss Julia tried to give her some rice soup, but she didn't want it — said she was too tired for anything but water. She had no appetite at all, and we didn't feel like forcing her.

It was the same with Maria. By Thursday she was having spells of delirium too. Several times during the night she woke me with her frenzied crying.

In the morning I found Mother lying on her back looking very old. Her eyes seemed small. She lay that way for the next few days, rarely stirring except for occasional periods of delirium or to ask for water. At times she lay as if wide awake, but she didn't hear a word I said. I didn't know what to do except pray. Miss Julia seemed just as helpless.

On Sunday, as I conducted the worship service I directed most of the prayers for Mother's and Maria's recovery.

Apparently word of their sickness had spread. That afternoon a Methodist lay preacher — maybe the only minister left in Effingham County — dropped by to see if there was anything he could do. I suggested he might pray for them, but he said he'd rather pray *with* them.

I told him, "You're welcome to pray with Maria, but I doubt that Mother'd hear a word you say. She just lies there with her eyes open."

"Can I see her?"

I let him in Mother's bedroom. "Mrs. Schmidt," he called, "do you hear me?" When he got no response, he said, "Maybe you can't talk, but just tap your finger and I'll know."

He pulled her arm out from under the blanket. "Good Lord!" he exclaimed. "I think she's got typhus. Seen it in the prisons enough."

"Typhus?" I asked anxiously, remembering that this is what they said Ned died of.

"Prison fever. Same thing. Have you had a doctor?"

"Where could we find one?"

"Umpf! Blamed war! Paper says Johnston's surrendering up in Carolina. Drat the war! All that killing, and what we all got to show for it? No doctors! Nothing! That's what!"

I grew irritated. "I don't care about Johnston or the war! Can you do anything for my mother?"

"I can pray for her. That's about all anyone can do now."

When he had finished his very loud prayer and driven off, I continued the prayer. "Please, God, please make them both well. You've *got* to!"

25. War Without End

Miss Julia consulted her remedy book. "Typhus — yes, here it is. 'Also known as cabin fever and prison fever.' If only we had known that before! 'Occurs most frequently in regions devastated by war.' Well, that fits us! Let's see. Remedy. Um. Hmm. Oh! Here we've been doing all the wrong things."

My sense of dread increased.

"We've got to make them eat," she announced.

We managed to arouse Maria sufficiently to take some soup, but with Mother we could do nothing. She was delirious again and knocked the soup away, spilling it all over herself and us. She kept mumbling, "Klaus! They can't take you! You're just a boy!"

I rattled the newspaper in front of her that Mrs. Mahlstedt had brought over. "He's coming home, Mamma! See? It's right here. A man from Augusta said they hadn't heard up there that Lee surrendered. They just found out. And now maybe Augusta will surrender. The man says he's sure they will. And that's probably where Klaus is. He can come home now. Do you hear me, Mamma?"

"Oh, Klaus," she mumbled, "don't go! They can't take you. Please, Klaus. You're just a boy. Just a boy."

I ran outside and yelled at the woods. "When's it going to end? The war's over! Over! But when's it going to stop killing?" Tag tilted his head and whined while a swirling cloud of dust played along the road as if to mock me.

Half delirious myself, I walked down to the church, sat on a charred pew before the half-burnt altar, and prayed. Then I fell on my knees amid the ashes and begged. When I was done begging I stood up and demanded: God *must* make them well! I had never talked to God like this before, but I had never wanted anything so badly before either. Father was dead and maybe Klaus too. Only Mother and Maria were left. God understood that. He had to!

I prayed until the sunlight had faded from the top branches of the pines. Then I got off my knees and went home. I found Miss Julia on the porch and asked, half expecting a miracle, "How are they?"

"Still delirious. Your mother's calling your name."

I went in. Simeon was standing beside her bed.

"I'm here, Mother."

"Think about it, Hans. Think about what I said," she mumbled, ever so weakly.

"I will, Mother."

"Think about what I said."

"I will, Mamma."

"Don't go, Klaus. You're just a boy."

Maria cried for water. I ran to give her a drink. She drank, then mumbled things I couldn't understand. She was still burning up. "Please, God," I prayed, "You've just got to make them well!"

In the morning I found Simeon sitting on the floor in one corner of Mother's room and Miss Julia in the other. They were both leaning against the wall, fast asleep. I sat on the floor and just watched Mother. She was staring at the ceiling. After a while she started mumbling again, causing Simeon and Miss Julia to wake up. At first her words were unintelligible, but then quite plain.

"Think about what I said. Just think about it, Hans." Then she started in about Klaus again. After that it was Father. "Why did you do it, Father? Why? You've always been against slavery. Why? A soldier. Why? Don't go. Don't go. I'm afraid. Please. Don't go! Oh, now I see you! It's all right." She quit tossing. Her face relaxed, almost as if she were going to smile. "Yes, You're all right. I see you. And you're with Jesus. I see Him. Oh, yes! I see Him too. He's coming. For me. Oh! It's all right. I . . . see Him."

"Mamma!" I cried, trying to shake her awake.

She went back to staring at the ceiling.

"It's the fever, Hans," Miss Julia said. "She's out of her

head. So don't you go putting stock in what she said. That's the way with fever."

I went outside with Simeon accompanying me. "When is she going to wake up?" I asked him.

"Don't no one know. It's up to the Lord. But He knows what's best. Your Father said so. Remember?"

"Yes, but . . . O Lord, please!"

I spent the rest of the morning with Maria. Once in a while she just looked dumbly at the ceiling the way Mother did, but not as long or often. At noon Simeon said, "No sense you staying here the whole day. You'll just worry yourself sick. C'mon. Us men folk'll go catch us some fish. The women folk can look after your Ma and Maria."

I wanted to refuse, but he was quite insistent. He led me way over to the landing by Jerusalem Church, talking the whole way in an effort to cheer me up. But as we passed the church cemetery, I started to cry and kept it up the rest of the way and even as we cast our lines into the river.

"Now, no need for all that. It's going to be all right."

"But when's my mother going to wake up?"

"You better mind your fishing or the line's gonna catch on that bush. You know, your Pa was one mighty fine man."

"Yes."

"Yessir, he treated me like a man."

"Uh huh."

"I was his slave too, belonging to the church and all. But he never said, 'Do this and do that.' Not that I minds work, but a man likes to do it free-like, and that's why there weren't nothing I wouldn't do for your Pa. Did you knows he taught me to read and write?"

"Uh huh. I mean, no." Tag snuggled his head under my arm.

"Well, he did. And when Mrs. Hanser found out, oh, she was fitting to be tied!"

"Mrs. Hanser? Really?"

"Oh, yes! She called the sheriff — Mr. Braun — and she

said, 'You git on and arrest that man.' And he says as how he'd have to, being as your Pa broke the law. Well, sir, that was, oh, about two days before your Pa got up in church and said he was a chaplain. And after church I heard Mrs. Hanser say she was gonna git the sheriff to fetch your father and put him in jail before he went off to the war."

"He never came by, I don't think."

"Sure 'nough, he didn't. He came by to see her, let's see . . . your father left on Thursday?"

"I guess so, I can't remember."

"Well, that there evening Sheriff Braun comes by and he tells Mrs. Hanser that now he's got time and he's gonna rush right over to the parsonage and throw your father in jail. Well, she knew your father was gone already to the train station, and she hollered and hollered and said, 'You git your bones down there to Savannah and catch him!' Well, Sheriff Braun he said, 'I ain't got *that* much time! I's busy.' And ooh-wee! Did she done turn the air blue! I never heard her call on the Lord before, except maybe in church, but she sure called on Him lots then! She was cussing and swearing. But the sheriff, he said he'd take care of everything. She says, 'What you gonna do?' And he turns to me and winks and he says, 'Don't you ever let me *catch* you a-reading.' And you know what? I never has!" At this Simeon just rocked with laughter.

I laughed a little too, then started to cry again. Even the sky began to cry, so we gave up our fishing and walked home in the rain.

Mother was still staring at the ceiling. I tried talking to her but she didn't even know I was there. Then she started coughing real hard like she had during the night. It scared me so badly that I ran outside and began to chop some wood. The rain was falling harder now and I was getting drenched, but the chopping drowned out the sound of her coughing.

Some time later Simeon came out and took the axe from my hand. "I'll see to that," he said.

He split a few pieces, then stopped, wiped the rain from his nose and said, "Remember what Miss Julia said this morning? About that not being your mother but the fever talking?"

"You mean about her not really seeing Jesus?"

"That's what I means. Well, don't you believe it. She saw Him."

"How do you know?"

He put his powerful arm around my shoulder. "I just felt it in my bones. She said the Master's coming to fetch her and take her to your father and the heavenly Father. Didn't she say that?"

"Well, yes, but . . . ."

"And it's true. 'Cause she's lying there real happy right now. He came and took her, just like she said. Just a few minutes ago."

I stood there trying to comprehend what he was saying. Then I screamed, "Mother!"

He held me back. "Stay. She's not there no more. She's happy with the Lord and with your father."

For some time he held me there in the rain — in the same rain that was now cleansing battlefields of their stains — in the same rain that was washing soldiers who were leaving behind the bleached bones of the unburied dead and were marching home with their swords sheathed. For them the war was over. But in their wake they had left unsheathed the swords of famine and disease to slaughter those of us who had survived. Where was the end? War! What I wanted once! And prayed for! What I wanted to visit on our enemies! The sword of war I had been so eager to draw had cut down Father. And now Mother. And now Mother! Who next?

When I was all cried out, Simeon said, "Let's go see Maria. She's the one what needs our prayers now."

First I *had* to see Mother. Tag lay on the floor, his head between his paws, looking at her. She was so still. I bent over her and whispered pleadingly, "Mamma? Mamma, I *need* you! Please, Mamma." I shook her lightly. "Mamma, please! I'm so alone. Please, Mamma."

Simeon lifted me from the bed. "You're never alone, Hans. Never. Remember that. Your father said so."

I wiped the tears from my eyes. "She looks so peaceful, Simeon."

"Yes, that's 'cause she's so happy now."

"So peaceful. She can't be dead."

"She ain't. She ain't never going to die no more. Remember? You read us about that on Easter."

He led me to Maria's room. I immediately put my arms around her burning body and cried. She was mumbling. Suddenly she screamed, "No, Mamma! Don't leave us. Don't leave us."

I gave her a squeeze as Miss Julia put a wet rag on her head. "It's all right, Maria," I sobbed. "Mamma's all right. I know that now. Oh, God, forgive me! He knows what's best, Maria. Mamma said so. And she was right. She's happy now. But God knows my heart will break if you go too. You're all I've got left. But it's all right, Maria. As long as you'll be with Him. It's all right, Maria."

I cried myself to sleep beside her. When I awoke, it was dark and Simeon was gone. Miss Julia said, "Why don't you go to bed, Hans? If the crisis comes, I'll call you directly."

"No," I said. "I don't want to sleep. I've got to pray. If she leaves . . . I want to be with her!"

In time I did fall asleep, and while I slept Simeon was doing for me those things I could never have done myself. He arranged for the Methodist preacher to conduct the burial service, he made a wooden coffin, and he dug a grave at the Ebenezer cemetery.

By morning all was in readiness.

The skies opened up a torrent of rain while by the great cedar at the near corner of the cemetery we laid Mother to rest. No hunger pain, no wound of battle could have hurt the way I hurt. But how much worse without Simeon!

Mrs. Mahlstedt walked home with me to where Miss Julia was caring for Maria. Simeon promised to come later — said he had something to make first, and my hurt beyond all hurts hurt even worse. "Oh, God," I thought, "please, not another coffin!"

I rushed into the house to see Maria. She was tossing her head from side to side, her eyes open but not seeing, her ears open but not hearing. I took hold of her arm. It felt like fire. I dipped my hand in the water and wiped it on her arm. "Please, Maria, not you too! O Jesus, forgive me. I'm a murderer and don't deserve anything, but please, if You can spare her! I've no one left. And help me. Your will is best. Help me to believe that, but I so want my sister."

All day long the rain drummed steadily on the roof. Just before dark it stopped and a mist crept out of the nearby swamps to brood among the surrounding pines. I could barely see Maria's face until Simeon made some torches from resinous pine knots and burned them outside her bedroom window. The flickering light danced over her lifeless face. Each time a knot burned out, I leaped forward to embrace her, so afraid that her life was going out too. But Simeon would light another torch and I'd sit back against the wall by Tag to watch and pray.

Once she called my name. I crawled over to her and answered, but she didn't hear me. I whispered, "If only you could hear me, just once anyhow! Maria, I love you. I've teased and haven't told you, but I do. Please, Maria, try to hear me. I love you. And if you go I don't know . . . I just don't know!" I cried and hugged her and wet the rag on her forehead.

Sometime during the night I must have fallen asleep. When the rooster's crowing woke me, light was already beginning to filter through the trees and a mockingbird was chirping in the oak across the road. I looked at Maria. She lay there with her eyes closed, as still as Mother after . . . .

"Maria!" I screamed, jolting Simeon and Miss Julia awake. "Maria! Do you hear me?"

Her eyelids twitched and she said weakly, "I'm thirsty."

Simeon felt her brow, then wiped his hand across it. He held it up. "It's wet!" he shouted.

I was so startled, I stammered in alarm, "Is this the crisis?"

He grinned. "No, that's done past now. Praise the Lord, she's on the mends!"

I felt her head. "It *is* wet, and she's not burning up anymore! And you *know* me now, don't you Sis?" I gave her a hard hug.

"Hans," she said, "I need . . . a drink . . . not . . . an old man."

"Imp!" I whispered, giving her a kiss. "I'll fetch you a pailful!" I raced out into the fresh spring air and with one long, joyous leap thanked God for giving me my sister back.

26. When Johnny Comes Marching Home Again

It was almost as if the war had never come to Savannah. Even in the late afternoon Wright Square overflowed with cattle for auction, and along Bull Street strolled prosperous-looking merchants with their top hats and walking sticks while a water cart wetted down the sandy street for the numerous carriages and wagons of commerce that rode by.

Business as usual. But for me nothing had gone right since that day two weeks earlier when Maria and I had packed our few possessions and moved in with the Mahlstedt's of Liberty Street, Savannah. I had looked for work at the rice mills, the gas works, the newspaper offices, the city market, the river wharves, the cotton warehouses. I had even tried to get a job driving one of those water carts. But to no avail.

As I turned right on Liberty Street I began to wish we had stayed in Effingham County. Mrs. Mahlstedt there and Miss Julia had both begged Maria and me to live with them, but I just couldn't picture myself being a planter. Besides I was getting old enough to launch out on my own.

I climbed the steps of the Liberty Street Mahlstedt's home. How grateful I had been to move in with them when we first arrived in Savannah, and how glad they were to have us at first, especially when I gave them the money for the ox and chickens I had sold! But now they claimed the money was running out. So was their hospitality.

"Hans!" Maria shouted, and ran and threw her arms around my waist. She looked up at me, and I could see more than love in her eyes. They teared with a mixture of fear, sorrow, and loneliness.

"I suppose you didn't find work again!" Mrs. Mahlstedt grunted.

"No, ma'am," I answered.

Mr. Mahlstedt laid his cup down on his saucer. "Seems to me you could find work if you really wanted," he said. "I don't think you're trying."

"I am, sir. I've tried every place you've suggested and more. Have you some other suggestions?"

He shoved the cup and saucer away from him. "That's what we get! Do my cousin a favor. Take you in for a day or two, and you take advantage of us. Just stay on and on, like we were made of money."

Maria squeezed me harder. "We gave you all the money we had," I said.

Mrs. Mahlstedt glared at me. "All the money that was left over, you mean!" She got up from the table, took off her apron, and slammed it on the chair. "Giving your house and land away! And to that darkie too — what's his name? Simeon? You could have sold it! But no, just give it away to a darkie and come poach off us!"

"Simeon saved us from starvation more than once," I said. "I wanted him to have a place of his own if the Hansers came back."

"And *we* haven't saved you from starvation? Ungrateful! That's what you are! Now I suppose you'll want to eat! 'He that will not work, neither should he eat.' That's what the good Book says. But you'll want to eat, I know."

"No, ma'am. I'm not hungry. Maria and I'll go down to meet the boats."

"Of course! Look for your brother! If you'd look for work the way you look for him, you wouldn't have to live off us! If it weren't for Mr. Mahlstedt's cousin . . . ."

Their remarks were blistering Maria's spirit, which had not yet recovered from her earlier wound. The shock of regaining her senses after the fever only to learn that Mother was dead and already buried had so greatly retarded her recovery that she was still weak. And she still smarted from the void Mother's death had created in our lives. How much abuse could our hostile hosts heap on her before her spirit would be beyond healing?

I took her down to the river to meet another boat from Augusta. Of course, we couldn't be sure that if and when Klaus returned he would return by boat. But the Yankees had torn up the railroad track to Augusta and it was too far to walk; so riverboat seemed the most likely way for him to come. Besides, meeting the boats got Maria out of the house and gave her something to think about and hope for.

As we pushed our way along the wharf through the ragged band of half-starved soldiers that had disembarked, Maria called out, "Klaus! Klaus!" But again no sign of Klaus. On the chance that maybe he had been captured and sent to a prison camp in the North, we went over to meet an ocean ship too, one of the first to enter the port through the recently cleared channel to the sea. Again no Klaus, and as we walked back to Liberty Street, Maria's spirit sank still lower.

Halfway through another day of futile searching for a job I ran into Pastor Koenig on Bay Street. It was like finding an oasis in the desert. He was working for a small printing firm now. When I told him about Mother and Klaus, he expressed surprise and sympathy and wanted to know how Maria and I were getting along. I explained that I was looking for work and about our situation with the Mahlstedts.

"If we had room, you could live with us," he said, "but we're just renting a few rooms. Still, you and Maria must come over one evening soon and have supper with us. Sunday evening. All right?"

"Yes, thank you, we'd like that."

"Let's not lose touch again. Tell you what. Every Sunday evening. A standing invitation. Here, I'll write down the address. Just maybe I'll find you some work too. Lots of merchants come to us for business cards and things like that. I'll ask around. Oh," he said, pulling out his watch, "I've got to get back to the shop! See you Sunday. Without fail. Right?"

When I told Maria about the invitation, she couldn't wait until Sunday. Nor could I, because by Sunday I was still without work and quite desperate. At the Koenig's Maria seemed cheered just to see a dinner table set with friendly faces. After we had finished eating, Pastor Koenig sat back, patted his paunch, and said, "Well, now that Mamma's meal has killed my appetite . . . ."

"The best meal in three years," I said. Mrs. Koenig smiled gratefully as if it were merely a matter of her superior cooking. "First hot biscuits almost since I can remember," I added, "and I'll bet Maria can't remember at all."

"Yes, that must be so," Pastor Koenig commented. "The war cost us years of good eating. Well, now about some work. You still need work?"

"Yes, sir. Do you know of anything?"

"Not yet, at least not for you, Hans. But let me ask Maria. Do you cook?"

"Oh, she's done more than enough of that," I answered, "though she hasn't had anything fancy to practice on!"

"Well, I know a man who owns a restaurant. A Jew, Mr. Winestock. At any rate, his cook ran off. So they need someone."

"Oh, but I can't ask Maria to work! She's still rather weak, and I'm to take care of her, not her of me."

Maria spoke up. "It's all right, Hans. I'd like to."

"Means a place to live if she can get the job," Pastor Koenig went on. "Living quarters go with it. Think about it. I'll write down the address. Know where Whitaker Street is?"

"Yes, sir."

"Meantime, I'll see if I can find you something, Hans."

"Thank you. I'd appreciate that." I looked at the address, then tucked it my pocket.

"You will think about it, Hans?"

"Yes, sir. I'll think about it. Oh, and there is another matter! The other day I heard that the trans-Mississippi states surrendered. And it's been a month since Augusta surrendered, so all our soldiers should be coming home soon."

"And Klaus too, you're thinking."

"Yes, sir. And we're going to have to tell him about

Mother, unless someone up in the county does first. Well, I just don't know how to."

"Of course. When he returns, whatever the day — or night, for that matter — you bring him here. Just leave it to me. But meantime you think it over about Maria."

Instead of going directly home afterwards Maria and I went to meet another riverboat, and another disappointment! That and the prospect of facing the Mahlstedts again so darkened her spirit that in spite of myself I promised to take her and Tag in the morning to see about the job.

The Winestocks' house was an elegant three-story brick affair with wrought-iron grillwork forming small walk-out balconies by the parlor windows.

Mrs. Winestock greeted us at the door. "So you're the girl my husband told me about! Don't you think you're pretty young to be a cook?"

"I'm nine years old, ma'am," was Maria's answer.

"Nine years old! Positively ancient! Why, you'd die of old age before getting a meal cooked! But I'll bet you really can cook. That's why I'm so sorry. But you see, I hired a new cook and butler just last night."

Tears gushed down Maria's stricken face so suddenly that Mrs. Winestock seemed taken aback. "Oh, dear, you're getting your shoes all wet!" Mrs. Winestock said, looking at the rags tied around Maria's feet. "Come in, my dears, dog and all."

She led us into the parlor and unwrapped Maria's feet. "Let's let your shoes dry out a minute. You know, my cook could use a helper in the kitchen. Yes, she's new and needs help. Do you think you could be a helper?"

Maria's face radiated the answer, so Mrs. Winestock led us through the dining room and hallway out the back stairs to the small courtyard formed by the house, carriage house, and stable.

"Up there," she said, pointing to the living quarters above the carriage house, "is where my cook Sheila used to live before she ran off with the butler. No-good Yankee trash filled their heads with all sorts of nonsense. Forty-five acres of good farming land for every slave family, they promised! And a bounty to get started on if the male joined their army! So my butler joined their army. Good farming land! Malaria-infested marshes on the coastal islands, that's where! Foolish child! She'll catch her death out there. Just didn't know when she was well off!"

From the courtyard Mrs. Winestock led us through a ground-level door under the house that opened almost directly into the kitchen. Maria's eyes lit up at the sight of the luxurious brick fireplace and the oven built into the chimney. "Well, child," Mrs. Winestock said, "here's where you'll be working. Now let me show you the rest of the place."

Beyond the kitchen sprawled a store room hung with cured meat and lined with bins of vegetables and shelves of canned goods. Mrs. Winestock opened the door at the far end of the store room. "In here's where you'll live," she said. "It was the butler's room. Needs some work, but if you're diligent you can make it quite comfortable. Definitely needs a woman's touch."

It needed something badly, but we were most grateful for anything right now.

"Hans, you can live here with Maria if you want. Your dog too."

"Thank you, ma'am."

"And you can eat meals with her too for . . . ." Her lips did some silent calculating. "How does four dollars a week sound to you?"

"Very fair, ma'am, only . . . ."

"Only what?"

"Well, at the moment I'm unemployed."

"Land of Goshen! Why didn't you say so?" She thought for a moment. "Maybe my husband could take you on at the restaurant, waiting on tables. Business hasn't been too good, though, the way the Yankees set the prices. Allow us to charge only 25 cents for iced drinks and ice cream. Can you imagine that?"

"No, ma'am. I can't imagine anything iced."

"Well, I'll talk to my husband tonight. All the other help are blacks, though." She looked at me questioningly, and I guess I looked at her dumbly. "That won't bother you?"

"No, ma'am. Should it?"

"No, I guess not. Would lots of folks, though. We're Jewish, you know, but I guess you knew that."

"Yes, ma'am."

"And you don't dislike us for it?"

"No, ma'am. I'm grateful to you. And envy you."

"Envy me? Why?"

"Because you're a blood relative of Jesus, and my father always said that that makes you quite special."

"Well, I suppose, except, well, I don't believe in Jesus as you do. Now do you envy me?"

"Yes, ma'am. It's just that you don't know how good He is, like I do."

"Hmm. A few more Christians like you and maybe I'd find out. Come, Maria. It won't do to have you wearing your bare feet around here. And, Hans, I'll talk to my husband tonight about that job."

The next morning I started to work as a dishwasher in the restaurant on Bay Street, and Maria showed the first signs since Mother's death of being happy. That evening when I read her the text of a speech by General Grant to his troops, she grew positively ecstatic. It said that the Yankee soldiers would be returning to their homes soon. We reasoned that this meant all Confederate prisoners would be returned home soon too. So on those days when we finished work early we continued to meet the boats.

As June wore away, though, arriving ships and riverboats brought fewer returning soldiers. By the beginning of July soldiers were arriving only in a trickle, and most of them were wounded. By mid-July one steamboat from Augusta had a total of one Confederate soldier aboard. I asked him about Klaus, but he said as far as he knew all Confederate soldiers in Augusta, both regulars and militia, had been paroled and sent home.

"Maybe Klaus is dead," Maria said and began to cry.

"He'll be coming home," I assured her, not believing it myself anymore. But on the way home I told her, "Let's not go there anymore. Klaus will come when he comes, and we can't hurry him by meeting the boats."

From the look she gave me I knew she knew what I was thinking. Well, what was the sense of pretending? It could only lead to further disappointment and dashed hopes.

I tried to keep her mind off of it by reading to her and giving her lessons in reading and literature. For the present I avoided history because it was too full of war, and Maria didn't need that — nor did I.

It was late afternoon early in August. I had the day off, and Maria was feeling crushed because the cook had scolded her for breaking a dish. So I said, "Why don't we make our quarters more liveable? Maybe we could buy some paint and fix up the room."

This excited her imagination. Soon she was erupting with all sorts of ideas for decorating — a plant here, a picture there, a yellow lamp by this corner, a blue rug before the door, and a thorough rearranging of the few articles of furniture.

"When can we start?" she wanted to know.

"Maybe Friday when I get paid we can shop for some paint."

"And material for curtains? I can sew them."

"Well, let's see how much the paint costs."

"Lavender curtains will make it so much prettier," she said, walking over to inspect the windows. "These just don't suit the place. And some bright paint. It won't look like a cellar any more. What color . . . ?"

She stopped so abruptly, with her mouth agape, that I rushed over to the window to learn the cause. Out front stood a carriage. Miss Julia and her husband, Mr. Brennen, were climbing down from it. Then I saw what had startled Maria.

She rushed out the back door, threw open the courtyard gate, and raced around to the front yelling, "Klaus! Klaus!"

I was beside her in a second.

"Maria! Hans!" Klaus cried. He dropped his blanket roll and gave Maria a huge one-armed hug. I grabbed his other arm but he pulled away as if trying to keep his hand in his pocket to hide a surprise.

When he let go of Maria, he gave me a hard, happy bang on the shoulder. "Hi, Hans," he said. None of us really knew quite what to say. We just looked at each other with silly grins. Tag jumped on him and wagged his tail furiously. "Hi, you old hound dog," Klaus managed at last.

Though Klaus had never had any weight to spare, he had lost quite a bit. His face, even smiling, was gaunt. Suddenly his face grew serious. He looked around as if to ask, "Where's Mother?"

"Where have you been so long?" I quickly inquired. "A prisoner?"

"No, nothing like that."

"Up in Augusta?"

"Yes."

"But the war's been over a couple of months now."

"Well, it's a long story. Sometime I'll tell you."

Mr. Brennen explained that they had spotted Klaus walking up the road from the old parsonage. They told him about our move to Savannah and drove him over right away. I thanked them and invited them in, but Miss Julia squirmed in her corset and Mr. Brennen pulled at his collar. They said it was a long way back home and they had to hurry. Before they drove off, I was able to get Miss Julia aside long enough to ask if they had told Klaus about Mother. No, she said, she didn't have the heart, and since Klaus didn't come right out and ask, they avoided the subject. This explained why they were so anxious to hurry away.

Inside Klaus grew quiet as he studied our quarters.

"They painted it an ugly gray, didn't they?" I commented. "But we're going to redo it."

He wandered past the beds as if noting there were only two. On the dresser he found the frame that held Father's and Mother's pictures. Before he could ask anything, I said, "We're supposed to go over to the Koenigs. We were just on our way when you drove up, but if you're hungry we could fix you a bite to eat on the way."

"No," he answered hoarsely, still keeping his right hand in his pants pocket. "I couldn't eat anyway."

As we walked along the street I chattered about the Winestocks and about my job. "Mr. Winestock said you can work there too," I added.

"No!" he snapped. For a minute he said nothing further, just continued walking with his left hand holding Maria's and his other hand tucked in his pocket. Then he said, "I'm sorry, Hans, but I don't want to wash dishes."

I switched the conversation to what he had been doing and why he had been so long in coming home, but he didn't want to talk about the war or himself. I told him about my being caught in a bombardment and about having to sell his violin, but he just grunted an occasional "uh-huh."

We walked the next few blocks in complete silence as fog rolled in from the ocean, wrapping the night in a mood as mysterious as Klaus's. I looked at each haloed lamppost up the street and counted them. Only six more to Pastor Koenig's house, and I was glad of that. I wanted to be there when Klaus asked about Mother.

"How's Mother?"

It came with such suddenness that my heart jumped. He had waited this long. Why couldn't he have waited just a little longer?

"Happy," I said, trying to evade the full truth.

"Good." We walked on past another lamppost. Only five more to go. "Is she staying at the Koenigs?" he asked.

"No."

He continued walking with head bowed and eyes on the wet stone walk. Four lampposts to go.

"Where is she, then?"

There it was. I had to answer. "In heaven."

He stopped. He didn't say a word or raise his head, just stared straight at the curb in front of him. A sob escaped from Maria's throat. Then he started across the street. He sniffed and with his free arm wiped his sleeve across his eyes. "I knew it," he said. "I knew it from the Brennens. Somehow I just knew it. And then when I saw you and the house." He walked a few more paces. "That's why I didn't ask."

I told him some of the details of how she died and also of how she had called for him.

Maria started sobbing aloud. Only then did Klaus break down and cry. And I cried.

When we reached Pastor Koenig's house, Klaus again wiped his sleeve across his eyes. "In a way," he said, "I'm almost glad. I didn't know how I was going to tell her."

"Tell her what?" I asked.

"Why I can't do dishes. And why I was so long in coming home. I needed time to heal."

"Heal?"

He pulled his right hand out of his pocket — I should say his right arm, because he had no hand.

"Oh, Klaus!" Maria gasped.

Quick as a wink I said, "But that won't stop a fellow like you, Klaus. Why, you can do more with one hand than a sea full of octopuses."

"Like washing dishes or playing a Bach suite for solo violin, I suppose? It'll keep me from doing lots of things. All the things I had my heart set on." He started crying again. "I'm glad Mother doesn't know, but . . . oh, Mother!"

As Pastor Koenig opened the door, my mind raced back to a day long ago. I could see myself parading along the road shouting, "We Georgians can lick the whole United States, the whole world!" War had seemed so exciting then. Now that we had had our war, what was to become of us?

27. Weird Noises in the Night

In our devastated land many a returning soldier had difficulty finding a job. This was especially true of Klaus. Mrs. Winestock let him stay with Maria and me, but throughout August he searched in vain for work. Then one evening early in September a stout woman came to see him. "I'm Miss Bungo from the Freedman's Bureau," she said. "Pastor Koenig tells me you need a job."

"Yes, ma'am."

"Well, we need workers. How would you like to teach school?"

"Teach school?" Klaus asked. "I don't know how to teach."

"But you can read and write and reckon, can't you?"

"Well, yes, of course."

"Then you can teach for us. You see, our bureau is trying to open schools for those, uh, unfortunate people who had been in bondage. The Savannah Educational Association has already opened schools for hundreds of colored children here in the city, but Chaplain Birge — he's in charge — he's supposed to open schools also on the coastal islands and in the interior, and already he's had to use many untrained teachers, practically any black who can read at all. Educational associations in New York and Boston are being asked to send teachers, but it will be months before they get here, and in the meantime we have practically no one to teach the colored adults. Folks here are opposed to our work or at least are too afraid to help because of their neighbors. We need people willing to teach these freedmen to read and write and do numbers — at least that much to start with. And Rev. Koenig tells me you'd be happy to see the colored people better themselves. Is that so?"

"Well, yes," Klaus stammered, "but I don't know . . . ."

"Please, Mr. Schmidt. So many people won't help us because we're, well, Yankees. Besides they want to keep the colored people ignorant. Will you help us?"

Klaus thought for a few minutes, then nodded his head.

As the days passed, his hesitation turned to enthusiasm. He felt useful again and needed, and I felt happy for him, little realizing what he and I were walking into.

For a schoolhouse the Bureau provided a large log cabin on the far end of a rice plantation about a mile west of the city. During the next few weeks Klaus planned lessons and tried to make the cabin at least roughly resemble what a schoolhouse should look like. On my days off I went with him to make some benches and a few needed repairs.

The opening day of school arrived. I wanted to go watch Klaus on his first day, but school began at 8 p. m., too early for me to get off from work. I was home, though, when he returned. He bubbled with enthusiasm as he explained that all the pupils were adult, some quite old, yet all eager to learn. One of them told him, "Learning gives white folk power. When we gets learning, maybe we can ride in carriages too and eat grandly."

The following night, though, trouble began. When Klaus reached the schoolhouse he found several pupils cringing in fear. They told of hearing strange, unearthly noises on their way to school.

This pattern was repeated every night through the week. Several pupils grew too frightened to venture out to school anymore.

When Klaus returned home Friday night he seemed especially troubled.

"What happened?" I asked.

"Someone nailed a chicken head to the school door. I don't mind telling you we all were nervous as a henhouse full of mice. But we went on with the lessons anyhow. Then it happened! We all heard these high wailing noises! One old man shouted, 'It's a spook!' I said, 'No, probably just some children trying to frighten us.' I went out to see but couldn't see a thing. It was darker than the inside of Mr. Wilkins's smokehouse. And the noises had stopped. But the instant I set foot back in the school they started up again. One student yelled, 'It's a hound from hell!' Well, I finally got the class back to order. But I can't figure out who's doing this or why."

"Why don't you report it to Miss Bungo?" I asked.

"I don't know. I guess it'll be a while before I can bring myself to report anything to the Yankees."

"Then don't go anymore," Maria begged.

"What else can I do?"

"Then Tag and I'll go with you Monday," I volunteered. "Mondays are slow at the restaurant. I'll talk to Mr. Winestock about it."

Mr. Winestock agreed to let me leave early Monday, so Klaus, Tag, and I set out together for the school. As long as we were sheltered by houses and lampposts, all seemed well, but beyond the city the moon bathed trees and vines in a spooky grayish-green hue, and ground mist swirled up in ghostly shapes on the canal and surrounding marshlands, making the whole landscape look haunted.

Less than half the pupils showed up at the schoolhouse. They told us they had heard those weird noises again but much louder than usual and had seen phantom-like shapes in the moonlight.

"It's not spooks or devils," Klaus explained. "Just frogs maybe, or crickets and ground mist."

"No, sir," one student replied. "We's heard them before. This was different."

"But still not spooks," Klaus insisted. "Maybe people, but that's all. Just people trying to scare you. Pay them no mind."

Klaus launched into the lesson as if nothing had happened, but no one paid much attention. He was teaching letters when all at once the noises started up.

"Oo-eeee! Oooh! Oooh! Oo-eeee!"

Many eyes darted wildly to the windows and back to Klaus and me. Tag's ears jumped to attention. I tried hard to appear calm, as did Klaus, and some pupils tried hard to ignore the noises too, but others couldn't take their eyes off the darkened windows or the door.

The noises stopped for a while, then started, stopped and started. Everyone's nerves were getting frazzled. Then once again all was quiet. The silence seemed almost worse than the eerie noises.

"Eee-yah!" The shriek came all of a sudden from right outside the windows. "Hoo! Hoo! Hoo! Eee-yah!"

Most of us bolted from our seats to the windowless wall in front of the classroom and huddled together. I was terrified. Most of the students were too, though a few looked defiant and ready to defend themselves against whatever it was that lurked out there.

The door sprang open! Students screamed, and Tag put his tail between his legs. Through the open doorway we peered into the black void outside, wondering, waiting, trembling.

Then they rushed in — about 10 men wearing masks. Most of them wore tattered Confederate uniforms. As threatening as these intruders looked, the students seemed to relax, as if glad to know they were up against only flesh and blood and not against ghosts or hounds from hell.

"Get out!" a tall man ordered the students in a thunderous voice that sounded familiar. Few of them obeyed. "Get out!" he repeated, waving a revolver.

"Where have I heard that voice?" I wondered.

Since most of the students had moved only a step or so, several of the masked men started shoving. "Get on home and don't you all ever come back! Hear?"

The students started to leave. As they filed out the door, the masked men pushed and shoved them along. "Hurry! Git! And no more notions about being good as other folk! Now git!"

After the last of the pupils was outside, one masked man fired several shots into the air behind them and let out a wild yell. The students started running.

The tall man with the familiar voice approached Klaus. "If you ever try to teach them niggers again, you're dead, hear? We've got no use for Yankee-lovers and carpet-baggers."

"But I fought for the South," Klaus protested. "Look!" He showed them the stump where his hand had once been.

The tall man knocked Klaus to the floor. "You're a traitor like your father!" he bellowed.

Tag snarled.

"Mr. Hildebrandt!" I gasped.

He punched me in the stomach, sending me doubled up to the floor. As I lay there struggling to catch my wind, a foot kicked me in the side. I heard Tag growling ferociously as if tugging on someone's leg, then a loud shot. The growling stopped.

"Well, I thought you might have forgot, but you still remember me, eh, Hans?" I looked up to see Mr. Hildebrandt, mask now removed, towering over me. "Then you know I mean business! I've got more than one score I'd love to settle with you. Remember?" That last word exploded from his mouth. And I remembered. "Don't you ever come back! Hear?"

Several men grabbed Klaus and me and threw us out the door head first. As I got up I looked around for Tag. I couldn't find him. Then I looked through the open door. He was lying on the floor in a pool of blood. One of the men poked his head out and yelled, "Now git!" and slammed the door shut.

"They shot Tag!" I called to Klaus. "Did you see? They shot Tag!"

"Yes, I saw."

"Why? Why'd they have to go and do that?"

As I walked along the tree-lined lane with my eyes filled with tears I bumped into a horse.

"That must be Mr. Hildebrandt's nag," Klaus whispered.

I wiped my eyes and looked. Yes, it was his saddle. Hildebrandt's. He shot Tag. My hands felt their way along the saddle, found the girth, and unfastened it. Then I stumbled away.

In a few minutes we reached the main road. We stood there awhile, trying to figure out what to do next. "They shot Tag," I said. "I'll get them for this!"

Suddenly I heard in the darkness behind me, *"Umpf!"* Then, "Who did it? Who did it? Hans Schmidt, you come back! I'll get you! Hear?"

We hid in the bushes alongside the road until they galloped past. Then we discussed what to do but couldn't agree. Klaus knew we could never get the class back without protection from Federal soldiers. Yet he couldn't bring himself to report the incident to them. "Working for the Yankees is one thing," he told me. "But reporting Confederate soldiers — I'd feel like a traitor."

"That's because Tag wasn't your dog," I said with determination.

The next day I reported the whole thing to Miss Bungo at the Freedmen's Bureau. She said simply, "I'll take care of everything. You just tell your brother to be ready to teach next Monday." And the set of her jaw told me she meant what she said.

Sunday night when Klaus, Maria, and I returned from supper at the Koenig's, we found the courtyard gate open. The door to the kitchen was open too.

"Who could have left them open?" Maria wondered. "The Winestocks are out of the city and won't be back till Thursday. And the cook and butler have the day off."

In our room we found the beds tipped over and the curtains torn down. Painted in big letters on the wall with the paint we had just bought were the words: THE YANKEES GOT HILDEBRANDT.

More words painted on the floor completed the message: NOW WE'LL GET YOU!

28. Again the Bugle Sounds

This time Klaus and I agreed on what we had to do. He and Maria hurriedly packed what little we had, while I hunted through the newspaper. "Be sure to pack my marbles and soldiers," I called, "and Father's buckle. Oh, here's something:

> Ho for Augusta! That light-draft Petersburg boat *Northern Star*, Charles Cousens, captain, will leave with dispatch for the above port. Report on time to Wight's Press or M. J. Doyle, 110 Bryan.

Maybe we can still book passage on the *Northern Star*."

We hurried down to the agent's office, bought our tickets, then hurried down to the boat and locked ourselves in our cabin until the boat was well under way. By the time we went out on deck, Savannah was no longer in view. In fact we were beyond the site of our one-treed island. But that raised a new worry.

"What if they saw us buying our tickets or getting aboard?" I asked. "They could've followed us."

"No," Klaus answered. "They would've been to our cabin before this."

"Yes, well, they could have ridden up to Ebenezer Landing and be waiting to board there."

"Worry-wart!" Klaus scolded. "We probably won't even put in there."

"Just to be safe, though, we'd better stay on the starboard side when we go by."

People came, looked us over, and passed by. None of them looked particularly threatening. Still, I didn't breath easy for many hours—not until we left Ebenezer Landing well astern.

That night we relaxed enough to start on some new worries. "What'll we do when we get to Augusta?" Klaus asked.

I was wondering the same thing as I watched the paddle wheel churn the black water into whitish foam. "Well, the von Rohrs said we could come back any time," I suggested.

"How can you want to go back there, after the revolver and all?" he answered.

"Got a better idea? Besides, he explained about the revolver."

A surprised look came over Klaus's face. "I thought you didn't believe him."

"Well, I didn't, but during war I guess you're ready to believe almost anything about anyone. Did you see him again while you were stationed there?"

"No, I avoided going anywhere near his place."

"Well, the war's over now. So what's there to worry about?"

Klaus snorted, "Indeed what! Remember me—Lefty? What kind of work can I find now?"

"Oh, you'll find something!" Maria said while adjusting her bonnet.

I wasn't so sure. And I started to worry about Maria too. She had never been to school. The little schooling Mother and I had given her wasn't very satisfactory. She needed to start, but that would depend on whether the von Rohrs would take us in.

"Yes, Klaus," I said without conviction, "you'll find something."

"And what are you going to do?" he asked. "Be a pastor?"

"Klaus, you've got more chance of being a one-handed violinist than me a pastor."

"Why?"

"Oh, you just don't know! You can't even realize . . . ."

"Try me."

So I told him about murdering the Yankee soldier. He said maybe it was the will of God, but I didn't believe that. God doesn't will us to kill each other.

"Maybe not," Klaus said, "but He does forgive."

"That doesn't make me fit to be a pastor."

"Well, a soldier then, like the Baron."

"In what army?" I scoffed. "The Yankee?"

Klaus and I fell silent, so Maria started chattering about Carl von Rohr. As the paddle wheels rhythmically churned the river, I found myself praying, "Lord, we don't know what to be or do. Surely You must have some plan for our lives. Help us. Show us. Please."

The von Rohr family welcomed us back into their home. In spite of all the devastation that had overtaken our land, they had prospered well. Within a week they had Maria in school and had helped Klaus land another job with the Freedmen's Bureau teaching a class of former slaves, and they found me a job in a poultry stall at the market in the middle of Broad Street.

Klaus fell so in love with his work that Mr. von Rohr promised to send him to college the following year so he could become a *real* teacher. And I made up my mind that one day I'd ask Mr. von Rohr if he had been the one who set fire to the warehouses — not that it mattered any more, but I was curious.

Meantime my problem continued. God had answered my prayer in part, showing Klaus what *he* was to be. But what about me? I couldn't believe I was designed to be a chicken huckster for the rest of my life. Yet the remainder of 1865 passed, also the first quarter of 1866, and I could find no answer.

Two days before my 18th birthday I talked the matter over with Mr. von Rohr as we walked among the pines behind the house.

"Seven years ago," I told him, "I was so sure. I swore I'd go back to Germany and be a soldier."

"Back to Germany? Seems childish now, doesn't it? But what about being a soldier? You always wanted to be like the Baron."

"The idea just doesn't charm me any more. War killed Father and Mother. Sam and Mr. Mahlstedt. And my friend Ned. And your son Frederick. It left Klaus with only one hand. And for what? To preserve slavery? It's gone. So the slaves can be free? Mrs. Hanser and a Yankee sergeant and my old schoolmaster have convinced me that won't happen in a 100 years."

"Well, when God's ready, He'll let you know what He wants."

I set off for work and prayed: "Please, Lord, Monday is my 18th birthday. Please show me by then — somehow — what You want me to be."

It suddenly occured to me with a deep sense of irony that there was only one thing I could be. A soldier. What I always wanted and never could be. And now that I didn't want to anymore, it was the only thing left.

Several blocks from the market I noticed a large number of people lining both sides of the street, looking up at the flagpole in the middle of the street. From it flew the Stars and Bars.

I hadn't seen a Confederate flag flying anywhere since the day the Yankees first marched into Savannah. For several blocks my eyes remained fixed on this apparition from the past, and my mind conjured up painful memories of those bleak war years. As I drew near a murmur swept along the line of spectators. Five Yankee soldiers: a second lieutenant, a soldier with a folded American flag, a bugler, and two color guards, came marching down the street. The young lieutenant was sputtering and fuming. He planted his hands on his hips as he faced off against the people on the other side of the street, then did an about-face to show us his exasperation. The crowd just laughed.

He marched smartly to the flagpole and without further ado lowered the Stars and Bars. He bundled the flag under his arm, then nodded to the soldier with the American flag. At this point someone in the crowd started to sing "Dixie." Others joined in, and by the time the bugler had the bugle to his lips the whole throng was singing.

It became a contest between the bugler and the crowd as the American flag was hoisted. In volume perhaps it was a tie, but not in persistence. When the bugler finished, the crowd started the song a second time and in a great surge of patriotic fervor rent the air with the majestic strains

> In Dixieland I'll take my stand
> To live or die in Dixie —
> Away, away, away down south in Dixie.
> Away, away, away down south in Dixie.

The flag detail stomped off utterly defeated.

The incident was trivial except for the way it prepared the events of the following day.

The von Rohrs, Klaus, Maria, and I started the day by going to church. Now, I knew that Rev. Heinrich, the new

pastor, was rather unpopular with some of the members. Whatever the deficiency was in this young man that made people dislike him, it was not a lack of preaching ability. In fact he sometimes disturbed me by the way his sermons kept me from sleeping.

This Sunday he was up to his usual habit. As he ascended the pulpit, I settled comfortably in the pew to take a nap. But then he intoned, "By this time surely you all have heard about the episode that took place yesterday morning on Broad Street. Perhaps some of you were there and took part."

I sat up and listened. "Perhaps," he continued, "it means that the spirit of patriotism which swept this land during the war years is not entirely dead. At least I like to think not. Those were noble years. Will there ever be their like again?

"What great burdens you bore then! What sufferings you gladly endured! What sacrifices you made! What heroic deeds you dared! You were surrounded by calamities but did not complain. You were overwhelmed by disasters but never surrendered to them. You embraced one another in a common cause and, setting aside self-interest, you became every man his brother's keeper — for the good of our land."

People thrust out their chins with pride.

"What shall I conclude? Indeed, what must God conclude? That war makes men noble? That men aspire to their very best when, and only when, they are engaged in shedding other men's blood? Why is it we become so dedicated when our acts of dedication create widows and orphans? Why is it we wax so inventive when it comes to creating engines of destruction? Why is it we are sheer geniuses in employing the arts of killing and maiming but sluggish and selfish in pursuing the paths of peace?"

People began to fidget, as if annoyed by his words.

"Think of what all you endured to defend our land,

though not only our land but also slavery, that peculiar invention of Satan that rightfully seared so many of our consciences! Can such dedication return even in this time of peace, even in the face of defeat?"

At the reference to slavery one man rose and noisily walked out of the church.

"It must have been a stirring moment down there on Broad Street, but can it be more than that — more than just a *moment?* Can it swell again from an occasional moment to a lifetime of dedication? Can it swell without the stimulus of combat? Can it swell from the love of God? Just for once from the love He bears toward us?

"If not from God's love, we are nothing but irrational beasts, bent on destroying and fit only to be destroyed. If not from God's love, this period of peace will be nothing but a pause in which we prepare new causes for fresh wars. If not from God's love, we will be using this peace to rebuild and realign those desires which we cannot satisfy but by further war."

The fidgeting in the seats increased.

"Many of you were soldiers in the recent war. You fought bravely for our country, and of that we all are proud. No sense of defeat will ever erase this pride from our hearts. But now we are living in a different time, and we need a different kind of soldier, with the same old courage but different nonetheless — God's kind of soldier."

Suddenly I had a feeling that through Pastor Heinrich God was speaking directly to me. Maybe it was the old charm of the word "soldier," I don't know.

"There are times, though perhaps rarer than we generally concede, when the issues are such that to choose the evil of war rather than submit to a monstrous tyranny is to choose the lesser of two evils. Five years ago we deemed ourselves to have entered upon such a time. So we chose to fight. If we judged wrongly, we leave that to God's forgiving grace. But choose we did."

Several people cleared their throats.

"The weapons we required then were weapons of destruction. But the weapons our poor land requires now are weapons of peace. It needs brave soldiers who will build a new land with justice and love, and who will heal our nation's wounds with the Gospel of Christ. Man or woman, youthful or aged, you can be such a soldier, Christ's soldier. Will you?"

After the service I heard some people talk about the terrible sermon by "that young, know-nothing meddler." But all day his words kept pulsing in my heart. I thought about "our nation's wounds." In my mind I saw that Yankee sergeant burning down Johnny's home. And the people looting the stores in Savannah. And Mr. Hildebrandt's masked men driving the Negroes out of the freedmen's school. And the stranger who killed an Indian only because he was an Indian.

I recalled also scenes of love: Simeon, who saved us from starvation; and Father helping a runaway slave; and the sheriff who didn't report him; and the church members who shared what little food they had. I began to realize that Jesus can make a difference in people's lives.

It also occurred to me that He had been a source of healing in my life—like the way He comforted me when Father died, and Mother. Surely He could also heal our land!

I went up to my room and studied the jar of marbles and the set of tin soldiers on my dresser. "Is this what You want of me, Lord?" I wondered. "Not a soldier like the Baron, but like my father?"

I felt almost certain of it, yet far from certain. Others He could use, but me? Hans Schmidt? The prankster, the disobedient son? The one who played mean tricks on Klaus, who cheated Sam, who murdered a soldier that had only charity in his heart?

Yet something inside me kept saying, "Yes, I want you."

Could God really be that forgiving? Was it He who was talking or just my imagination? How could I be sure? No matter what Mother and Father had said, I just couldn't picture myself as a minister. I prayed again: "Heavenly Father, if this is really Your will, show me. I don't even know how to become a minister. If You want me to be Your soldier, then let Mr. von Rohr show me what I must do. Then I'll know this is what You want."

I went downstairs and told everyone I was thinking of becoming a minister. "I'm just thinking, mind you. I'm not at all sure," I hedged.

Klaus and Maria were delighted with the idea. Mr. von Rohr rubbed his jaw, then said, "If that's what you want, Hans, we'll help you. You'll have years of study ahead, but in the fall we'll send you to Newberry College in South Carolina, if the war hasn't destroyed the place. Meantime I'm sure Pastor Heinrich will help you get started on your studies. And we'll see you through college, also the seminary at Lexington."

Mr. von Rohr had not only showed me what I must do but also was willing to make it possible! That seemed to settle the matter. I went back up to my bedroom and said, "Lord, if You can use someone like me to do Your work, You're even more wonderful than I ever dreamed." But I still had serious doubts. Something just didn't seem right.

I went over to the dresser and looked at the tin soldiers, 10 reminders of my long-standing determination. Practically everyone I knew had been a soldier, even people who had never wanted to be, like Klaus and Father. Mr. Mahlstedt had been one, and John Kraft and Sam and Ned. Even Mr. Hildebrandt.

The door banged behind me, giving me such a start that I knocked one of the soldiers off the dresser.

"I'm sorry," Klaus said, "I didn't mean to frighten you."

He picked up the two halves of the soldier. "Maybe I can fix it with some heat."

"That's all right. I can fix it."

"But you just can't get over the idea of being a soldier, can you?"

"No, it's . . . it's just that everyone has been one. They've proven their courage. Like you. And I'll never know whether I have courage like the rest of you."

"Courage?" Klaus laughed. "Do you think this is a result of courage?" He held up the arm missing a hand. "What do you picture? That I heroically manned some rampart against the vicious onslaught of the enemy?"

"Well . . . ."

"Listen, Hans, there was no enemy and no rampart. A riot broke out here in Augusta, and somehow some little street urchins got ahold of firearms. I was just standing around on Broad Street when it broke out. Some shooting started and we were all running this way and that. And that's when I got shot. By a kid no more than 12 years old. He didn't hardly know what the gun was for. But the real damage was done by an army surgeon. Courage? Believe me, if I had a choice I would have run from that butcher!"

"All right, but there were others, lots of others."

"The others were the same. I talked to enough of them. I know. You think they're like your painted tin soldiers: colorful, glamorous, silently courageous when they fall — like this piece of tin. But they're not. When they get hurt they feel pain and bleed and scream and cry for their mammas."

"Yes, well, at least they don't run away. They risk the pain and suffering. That's their courage."

"You're right, most of them don't run away even when they're scared to death, but it has nothing to do with courage. Just maybe it's the ones with courage who run. Do you know what keeps men from running away when they're scared to death? Not courage but fear. They're afraid of being laughed at or scorned by the other soldiers or by their families and sweethearts. They're scared to death of what people will think of them. They're more afraid of that than of pain or even dying."

"You're trying to tell me they act brave in the face of the enemy because they're really cowards?"

"That's about it. But you want to know who's really got courage? The person who will stand up for what he believes in, even when people laugh at or think evil of him for it. Of all the heroes of the battlefield few of them have this kind of courage. But you saw an example of it this morning."

"You mean Pastor Heinrich?"

"Yes. He knew the members well enough to know what would happen if he preached that sermon. But he had more courage than a whole army of soldiers — the kind of courage Father had. I know you think Father's courage started the day he went off to war. Believe me, he was a brave soldier long before that. Remember when he stood up to the Hansers or helped the runaway? Hans, you don't need to be a soldier to show courage."

I looked again at my painted tin soldiers, then at Klaus with a bit of wonder. "When did you get all this wisdom?" I asked.

He grinned. "I guess it must be a shock to find that your older brother isn't a complete idiot."

I turned the tin bugler over in my hand. "How wrong can I be! Somehow I always thought of my life as heading toward the sound of the bugle."

"Maybe it has, only the bugle was sounding a different call from what you thought."

Thus it came about that I went to Newberry College, not far from Columbia, South Carolina. And thus it happened that in my third week there a Negro coachman delivered a letter to me in my dormitory room. It read:

"Lieber Hans,

We were delighted to learn only today that you are studying here at the college. It has been so long since we have seen you. Would it be possible for you to have dinner with us next Sunday noon?

Please send word with the coachman. On second thought, we would be overjoyed if you could come with the coachman now and deliver your answer in person. I hope I am not betraying a trust in saying that our Sally Jo insists it has been so long a time that to extend it another week would be an atrocity.

With most affectionate regards, I remain,

Anna Klug.

I rode with the coachman and plied him with questions while I finished fumbling with my shirt and tie.

"Oh, Miss Sally Jo?" he said. "She's pretty as a picture and lively as a grasshopper. Hardly bigger than a flea bite, but she's all lady. She sure is."

We rode on for a few minutes in silence, and I gave a tug on my belt. The coachman noticed the buckle.

"You was a soldier?"

"No, it was my father's."

"He was a soldier?"

"Yes. He's dead now, though."

"Oh, I'm sorry! What was your daddy before the war?"

I thought for a moment. "I guess he was always a soldier."

"You going to be a soldier like him?"

"Yes, like him."

"Oh, I bet if he was alive he would sure be happy to know that!"

An autumn breeze rippled the dry leaves overhead. And suddenly a feeling came over me that — somehow — Father did know and that he was happy indeed.

Concordia College Library
Bronxville, NY 10708

PRO
DAN   PRINTED IN U.S.A.